MW00916443

LAST TRAIN HOME

The American West Series

LAURA STAPLETON

Text and Cover Image Copyright © 2019 Laura L Stapleton

Cover by Cheeky Covers

Edits by Aquila Editing

All Rights Reserved.

No portion of this book may be reproduced, stored in a retrieval system, or transmitted in any form or by any means, mechanical, electronic, photocopying, recording, or otherwise, without written permission from the author or publisher.

Names, characters, and some incidences are imaginary and complete fiction. The places are real whenever possible, and some geographical names have been changed since the story took place.

To Liberty, Tom, Carter, and Conner.

ACKNOWLEDGMENTS

Huge thanks to the National Orphan Train Museum in Concordia, Kansas. The train depot housing the museum is exactly what I imagined while writing this story.

CHAPTER 1

Jack Dryden stared out the dirty window, chin resting on his hands as if in prayer. He shivered. The midmorning sun barely affected the frost. Last night's fire in the woodstove remained cold and silent behind him. His wife, Ellie, had been gone three weeks, or was it four by now? His days blended into one blur since she'd left.

He did happen to remember the orphans arrived today. Sending a letter canceling the adoption hovered at the top of his chores. Yet Jack didn't have the heart to even write the message, never mind the ride to town and send it. "You picked a hell of a time to leave," he growled, as if she'd hear him while at home in Boston.

The papers lay on the table in front of him and reflected the morning light from the window. One's handwriting held the graceful curve of his runaway wife with a formal and final goodbye. The page covered a divorce decree for him to sign. His gut churned yet again. Wives didn't divorce their husbands. He'd meant it when vowing until death do them part, even if she hadn't.

Jack scratched the back of his neck. Their love might have faded to tissue-thin over the years, but he still respected his wife. He folded both papers, his signature blank, vacant and nagging at him. After a couple of seconds, he tucked in the envelope flap. Ellie had left because of him and not for anyone else. He reckoned neither one of them was in a hurry to make the document final.

The typewritten notice of the instant family he'd requested several months ago now sat on top. He sighed. No need to rush over to the courthouse after telling the orphans he'd not be able to adopt them after all. He had enough bad news to deliver already. Unable to leave it alone, Jack pulled the official letter from its envelope and stared at the enclosed photo.

The Children's Society had sent the information about the girl and twin boys soon after Ellie's departure. He narrowed his eyes. If she'd waited a couple of weeks to leave him, the orphans and his wife might have passed each other on the way to the children's new home. Jack wondered what Ellie might say if seeing them in a depot while they waited for the train to him. What could she say? "Sorry, but I'm not your mother or your father's wife after all"? Judging by her goodbye letter, Ellie wouldn't have the guts to say the words. He snorted. Maybe pin a note to their lapels, but that's all.

He looked over the photo, not bothering to reread the date written on the back. The sadness in the children's eyes told him everything. The girl stood behind the boys, a hand on each of the twins' shoulders. Jack couldn't help but smile, recognizing the protectiveness of an older sibling. In the image, the trio seemed well taken care of, and maybe they had been before their parents' deaths.

Jack slid the photo back into the envelope. A black and white image said nothing about hair or eye color, but the nuns had waxed poetic about the blonde hair and blue eyes of all three and how lucky he was to get such beautiful children to raise. He grunted and pushed aside both letters on the table. A person's looks didn't matter to him right now. Ellie proved to him that a pretty outside never meant a pretty inside.

He stood, the chair's legs scraping along the dusty wood floor. The place wasn't ready for more than the meager livestock he had, never mind new family members. Jack grabbed his coat and hat on his way to the door. He'd ride into town, tell the nuns he couldn't take the orphans after all, and be done with the matter. Maybe live another year out here and get the homestead ready to sell. No need to stay and build a family farm when Ellie had taken his heart back to Boston.

Once outside, a hard breeze cut through his coat. The early winter sky's pale blue matched the icy air. Jack hoped his horse, the one Ellie had left him, would move better in the cold than he did.

He walked up to Shep's stall in the barn and paused. The animal nickered, and Jack grinned. "Hey boy," he said, coming up to the animal and running a hand along his neck. "Feel like going into town?" As if answering him, the horse nudged his arm. Jack chuckled and said, "All right. Let's go." He led Shep out of the stall.

The buggy sat to one side of the wagon, and he paused. Riding would be faster, but he might need more than saddlebags after stopping by the dry goods store on his way home. "I suppose hitching the buggy wouldn't hurt," Jack muttered and reached for the bridle. "It'll keep me from visiting the saloon for some Christmas cheer, right, buddy?" The horse nickered when Jack gave him another scratch between the ears. Some men left their wagons tied to the post outside the saloon in any weather. He'd wanted to unhitch all the suffering animals and care for them like they deserved.

He soon had the horse fastened up and ready to go. Leading the animal past the house before getting onto the wagon reminded Jack he might need the orphanage's letter after all. "Give me a minute, boy," he muttered and hurried into the house to scoop up both letters. Ellie's goodbye would be proof to the caretaker that the children would be better off with anyone but him. He shoved the envelopes into a coat pocket.

His footsteps on the frozen blades of grass almost drowned out the papers' crinkling as Jack went to Shep. He double-checked the rigging and planned to reread Ellie's goodbye one more time before writing a final plea for her to return home to him. He paused for a moment before digging leather gloves out of his other coat pocket.

A contrary voice inside of him piped up about how she'd refuse him yet again. A smart man would have the papers signed and delivered by now. He shook his head, intent on dealing with the divorce later. Once on the buggy seat, he clicked to Shep. "C'mon, boy. Let's get this over with."

ALICE McCARTHY SQUEEZED THE HANDBAG'S handles. Her first trip so far west to Liberty, Missouri, couldn't go awry now. She glanced at the eldest child,

Charlotte, and smiled in reassurance while saying, "Mr. Dryden will be here soon. We're early, that's all." Worry faded from the girl's blue eyes, and her shoulders relaxed.

Charlotte shifted her belongings to the other hand and wrapped a blonde curl around her now freed finger. "I hope so. They do want us, don't they?"

"Of course, they do," Alice assured her. She kept a watch over the twins as they played tag around the railroad depot's rosebushes. Charlotte's twelve years to the boys' ten wasn't a huge age gap, and she smiled. Their difference in maturity meant the girl paced from nervous energy with her instead of dirtying her clothes while playing. Alice took a couple of steps toward the edge of the train station platform, and said, "Boys, be careful to stay neat. We want to impress Mr. and Mrs. Dryden, not scare them."

"Yes, Miss McCarthy," they chanted in unison. One of them wiped dirty hands on his pants, leaving limestone-white streaks on dark fabric.

"Oh, Conner." Alice sighed and reached for her handkerchief. "Come on over and let me clean you up. The Drydens should be here at any moment."

The boy did as she requested with Carter following him. Charlotte dropped her bag next to her brothers' and crossed her arms while tapping her foot. Alice hid a smile at how well the girl mimicked Sister Theresa's mannerisms. Good thing they weren't in the Children's Home at the moment, or the Sister might take it personally.

"There." Alice gave his trousers a final swipe of her handkerchief. "All better." She straightened. "Be careful to not let the thorns snag on anything."

Neither boy replied but ran back to resume their game. She shivered and turned to the young girl. "Let's walk around again to keep warm."

Charlotte nodded, and both picked up the boys' carpetbags. The two stepped off the platform and into the winter sun's warmth. Alice checked the time on the depot's clock before they turned the corner. They'd been here two hours with no Drydens. People backed out of taking in children all the time. She'd have to contact the town's children placement board members at some point. Let them make suggestions on the best parents for the Hays children.

She chewed on a small chapped piece of her lower lip. Alice had reviewed the Drydens' application herself, along with acquiring Sister Theresa's final approval. So many people needed help on the farm, and the couple seemed like reliable, decent folks. Not the type to miss meeting new family members for the first time.

Neither woman hurried for the shady side of the station, nor did she and Charlotte talk. While the girl was naturally quiet, Alice wanted to stall chatting with her about putting the three of them up to the community at large. Give the prospective parents a little while longer, just in case.

"They're not coming for us, are they?"

She paused in mid-step at the girl giving voice to Alice's worries. "Oh, I wouldn't say that. They might be delayed for some reason. The farm is a half-day's ride, remember."

Charlotte nodded, and they continued walking to the far side of the depot and out of the warmth. "I'd like to believe that, but it's late afternoon."

"I know. Everything will be fine, I promise." She smiled, ignoring the guilt smothering her heart. Alice could guarantee nothing, really, except she wouldn't abandon this family. The sisters at the Home encouraged keeping siblings together, but sometimes separations couldn't be helped. She glanced at Charlotte. She had shifted to holding everything with one hand and toyed with her hair again. The girl had a curl wrapped around her index finger so tight, the skin was a reddish purple. Alice shared her fear and placed a hand on her slight back. "Even if the Drydens have changed their minds, you're not to worry. I'm here to help you and the boys find a good home."

They turned the corner, and both halted when seeing the boys hugging a man as if they were never letting go. When he glanced up at the ladies, Alice's heart stopped as she stared into the greenest eyes she'd ever seen.

The mystery man had several days' beard as black as his midnight hair. A hat pressed low over his forehead gave him an intense appearance, even if the dark curls hinted at the more boyish aspect of him. His clothes looked a little too lived in, and she wondered what wife would let her husband go to town in a rumpled shirt and pants. His coat and boots had some wear as well.

Finished with her appraisal, she glanced up into his eyes again. His slight smile led her into giving him one of her own. He awkwardly patted each child on the back, his expression silently begging her for assistance. Alice swallowed and took a step forward. "Hello, it looks like you need some help."

The twins flanked him, holding on as if he were a tree during a hurricane. He gave her a slight grin. "I do, please," he responded while putting a hand on each boy's shoulder.

The man's deep and even voice did fluttery things to her heart, and her face filled with heat. She'd met so many men in the past year of helping children find homes. This one beat out anyone she'd ever met before, and Alice cleared her throat to collect herself. "This raucous behavior won't do, boys." What if the couple showed to take the children home and saw them clinging to strangers? "Come along. Let the gentleman go."

Before she could step up and pull the twins away, Charlotte squeaked out a sob. "Pa? Is that really you?"

CHAPTER 2

JACK'S BLOOD POOLED IN HIS FEET AND LEFT HIM lightheaded. He wasn't anyone's pa. Not yet, anyway, and not until the Hays children arrived. Two boys and a girl stood next to one of the loveliest women he'd ever seen. "No, I'm sorry. Wish I was, but no," he croaked.

The girl shook her head, tears filling her eyes, and the boys clung to him tighter. "I suppose not," the young girl said. "You fit the description, that's all."

The woman with the deluded youngsters stepped forward. "Here, boys, let go of the gentleman." She tugged at their shoulders, and after a little resistance, they complied. "Pardon us, please. We're expecting the children's new parents, and they're a little overexcited."

His neck stiff with tension, Jack tried to give her a curt nod. Telling the children how they'd have to turn around and go back to a place they couldn't call a home broke his heart. Anyone would be eager to begin a better life, and he responded, "I can't say I blame them. A new life out west is always exciting."

"I'm glad you understand." She shifted from one foot to the other before asking, "Although, how did you know we're from back east?"

"Most people around here are somewhat tanned by the sun. Not the ladies so much, but everyone else can't help it." Jack smiled and held out his hand. "I have to confess, though, I'm Jack Dryden and pretty much know Charlotte, Conner, and Carter from the photo."

"Oh," she replied, her voice soft as she shook hands with him. "I'm Alice McCarthy. Pleased to meet you."

"Same here, ma'am." Jack reached out to greet the boys with a handshake, too. "Pleasure to meet you both." He smiled at Charlotte. "Young lady."

The girl shook his hand with a small smile. "Likewise, Mr. Dryden. Will your wife be along soon?"

Now would be when the cow patty hit the ground, Jack reckoned. There'd be no way to pretend Ellie hadn't been eager to meet her new children. A less honest man would say she'd stayed behind at the farm. Tell Miss McCarthy she could go on home and leave with the Hays-turned-Drydens. Get everyone back at his place before confessing to his newly created bachelorhood so the instant family would have to stay with him.

He rubbed the back of his neck. A lie never solved anything. Eventually, someone from the adoption committee in town would visit or get wind of his wife leaving him. Clearing his throat, Jack turned to Alice and said, "About Mrs. Dryden. We should probably have a talk before deciding anything else."

She glanced at Charlotte and the boys before responding, "What do you mean?"

Jack faltered for a moment since saying the words made her leaving real. "Ellie's gone, for good, and that's why..." His words trailed off as the quartet's expressions changed to dismay and confusion. "I won't be able to adopt as we'd planned." He looked from Alice's narrowed eyes to Charlotte's trembling chin to the boys' clenched jaws and fists. His nose stung. "I'm sorry."

Alice frowned as Charlotte fell into her arms, quietly sobbing. "Very well. A couple can change their minds. I suppose instead of being angry you waited until we arrived to tell me, I should be glad you mentioned your refusal just now."

Carter wiped his eyes with quick, sharp motions. "You look like our pa but don't act like him."

"Our pa would've adopted us no matter what," Conner added with a pout. "He was a good man."

Carter nodded, frowning. "We didn't have a mother after we were born and did just fine with a father."

Alice tsk-tsked and shook her head. "Boys, he has a right to change his mind. If you all had refused to go with him, I'd have to respect your wishes, too." She lifted her chin, staring down her nose at him as much as a shorter woman could. "Thank you, then, Mr. Dryden. If you'll excuse us, I have to arrange our lodging for tonight and begin to find homes for the children tomorrow."

More than one home? Jack had heard about the families split up when a couple only wanted one or two children out of several. The sadness in their faces matched the sorrow in his heart. He'd wanted this family with Ellie. She might have left for good, but nothing said he had to let the children go, too.

He clenched his fists before saying, "Don't, please." Alice turned to him, her face as chilly as the air around them as

Jack faltered. "I mean, let's go inside the depot where it's warm, and discuss everything before you try to place the children elsewhere."

Alice nodded. "Very well." She gave a final pat to the girl's back and led them inside. "I suppose a few minutes won't hurt."

Hope grabbed his heart, and he grinned. He had a toehold and could persuade more time out of her. His horse would need care first. "Be right there." Jack hurried to Shep, tying him to the hitching rail before petting his nose. "Wish me luck, buddy."

He walked to the building, now golden in the winter's slanted sunlight. Bare tree branches behind him cast long shadows up the side of the depot. Hand on the door, he paused. What would he say? Tell them to come home with him? To a motherless house in desperate need of a scrubbing? Jack had added a couple of bedrooms this fall, planning for today. Now, his efforts didn't seem to be enough.

Spending a winter with the children would be fun, but spring? Warmer weather meant new crops, new livestock, and lots of problems two boys could cause without a woman's steadying hand on them while Jack worked. He turned the handle, ready to give up the children for their own good.

The door hinges creaked, and he stepped in to find the quartet staring at him. Every one of them frowned. He tried his most charming smile and stepped up to them. "I know you're worried about being separated from each other. That's my worry as well." He eased his hat off his head, resisting the urge to crush the brim in his hands. "With that, I plan on working with Miss Alice here and find you a good home."

"Why don't you take us in?" Conner asked. "We can write to Mrs. Dryden and ask her to come back."

"It's not that simple." He looked at Miss McCarthy for help in convincing the children he'd be inadequate as a single parent.

She put her arm around the boy. "He's right, Conner, and has made his decision." Alice glanced at Jack before continuing. "I realize this isn't what we expected or wanted, but Mr. Dryden does have the right to change his mind, remember?"

Charlotte stared at her feet. "He wanted us until we met him."

Carter stepped up to him, toe to toe. "That's right. He doesn't like us, but is too chicken to come out and say so."

The hairs on the back of Jack's neck bristled like the feathers of a banty rooster ready to fight. "I am not afraid to say anything, young man. I like you three just fine, but you deserve a mother, too. That's all."

Alice gently pulled the boy back. "Children, please. Have a seat while he and I talk about our options." None of the youngsters moved, and she patted the twins on their shoulders. "Go on. Occupy yourselves while we find a solution."

The three shuffled off to the nearest row of seats and sat, glaring at him. He leaned in to say to Alice, "I hope you understand. These children need more than a father."

"I do." She moved to his right, turning him away from a line of sight toward the Hayses. "You're aware of how the boys only ever knew one parent. Their mother died in childbirth with the twins. Charlotte was too young to remember her, and their father raised them until earlier this year."

He nodded, remembering the slight biography he'd read about them. "I know." Jack stared at the wall. He hated Ellie for leaving him and now their family. If he'd been able to convince her to stay, no one's heart would be broken right now. As it was, he'd have to teach his former wife's chores to the trio while somehow accomplishing his own.

Jack glanced over at the kids. Charlotte sat like a proper little lady. Carter swung his feet, making swish sounds when the shoe soles connected with the wood floor. Conner had his elbow on an armrest, holding up the side of his head with a hand. He'd fallen for them by the second letter, wanted to be their father, but not without a wife. He sighed. "I can't raise them alone."

Alice looked down at the floor, her lips set in a thin line. "You'll get no argument from me. However, I'd like your help in finding a good home for them." She glanced at the trio before continuing. "Preferably together, but two families in the same town would be best." She turned to him with a shrug. "I'm loath to separate the twins but can if we must."

Jack searched her face, her calm, unruffled face. His churning gut didn't match her calm attitude. The idea of packing each of the Hayses off to live without the other two seemed too cruel to bear. How could anyone who cared for children do such a thing to them? He wanted to shake some sense into her. "You're willing to place them in separate homes, miles apart if necessary?"

Her composed mask of a face slipped into a brief fury before she said, "If needs must, Mr. Dryden. Only a few of our children have been taken in by families in different states, but we do need to accept whoever can provide a stable and loving home."

"I..." he began before trailing off. No, he couldn't blame the orphanage for doing what they must under challenging circumstances. They relied on private donations and the kindness of strangers. He turned and watched as Charlotte dabbed her eyes and hugged her brothers a little tighter. His heart squeezed in his chest like her arms did around the boys.

He couldn't do it. He couldn't send them anywhere and break up what was left of their family. Not only did they need each other, but he needed them, too. He refused to let Ellie take away all his future with her leaving. "You're not separating them."

"Excuse me?"

Jack didn't look at her but smiled at the children when they looked at him in amazement. "You heard me. You're not separating them because they're coming home with me."

CHAPTER 3

ALICE'S JAW DROPPED FOR A MOMENT BEFORE SHE laughed at his audaciousness. She might be young, but she didn't answer to anyone but the sisters and Father O'Brien when it came to her and the children. She put her hands on her hips. "I'm sorry, but I have a duty to fulfill, and I don't take orders from you."

He lifted his chin as if she'd punched him and crossed his arms with a scowl. "Not orders, ma'am, just a serious suggestion."

She looked him up and down, inspecting him and his sincerity. His frown eased a little, and she tried not to smile. Jack didn't fool her with his bluster. Alice sensed and shared the concern he had for the Hays children. She just wasn't sure if she could share the responsibility for them with him. The Home did encourage its agents to keep families together. "Maybe so."

Jack grinned, and Alice's heart did a little flip over how handsome he was. She couldn't be sure if Ellie Dryden was a fool for leaving such a fine man. The woman might have been wise to escape a bad situation. She owed it to the children to dig a little and learn more before considering his recommendation. "I'm open to the idea of you being a father. Tell me more about this sudden change of heart."

Jack shrugged and looked down at his feet for a moment before glancing at the children. The trio stared back at him. He gave them a wink and said, "Ellie was a city girl when we married. If I could teach her how to farm, I can teach those three as well." He smiled at Alice. "Besides, they're a family, and I want to keep them together."

"With you?" she blurted before catching herself. Of course, he meant to be their father. Alice shook her head at her foolishness. Every time Jack smiled or seemed sad, every bit of her professionalism evaporated.

Before she could say anything else, he said, "Yes, with me, because I won't have anyone else. We need each other."

An image of him alone at some random homestead flashed in her mind. He still must be broken-hearted over Ellie leaving him. She wasn't unused to feeling alone in the world and swallowed the beginning lump in her throat. "Very well."

He grinned and took a step toward her. Alice's heart skipped a beat, and she ignored the flutter. Her voice rang out a little loud as she said, "I'm willing to visit your farm, inspect it, and possibly place the children with you." She glanced over at the Hayses, each young face gleaming with hope. "Don't expect me to be lenient, but I will be fair."

He clapped his hands once before giving a grin to the children. "Good enough, Miss Alice. We can visit one of the board members now. Petition them to speak on my behalf."

"Do they know about your wife?"

His smile fading, Jack's lips thinned into a grim line. "No. Not yet. I saw no reason to squawk about her going home."

Her superiors wouldn't be happy at the lie by omission. Yet Alice couldn't blame him, understanding the need to protect his ego. "What happens when they learn she's not here?"

Jack stared past her. "I'll deal with their questions when that happens. Until then, I can take care of the children until you see fit to let me adopt them for good."

"Alone?" she asked, and when he nodded, Alice shook her head. "I don't like the idea." His prior family life wasn't coming to mind at the moment. She had read so many applications since going over his. "Have you ever cared for siblings before now?"

Jack led her over to a bench and sat when she did. "Yes, my brother and sisters. I was the oldest of four."

"Ah, an excuse for your imperious nature," she said while setting her travel bag to her side. Alice faced him for further questioning and returned his sudden grin. Her heart did that skipping thing again, and she had to confess he had such lovely features for a man. "I'm assuming you were the ringleader of any mischief?"

"Yeah, I'd boss them around, and they'd ignore me."

"Well," she began before glancing at the children. All of them were watching intently, none of them seeming happy. Alice couldn't blame them. She had to decide their fates before going back home. If they stayed and came to harm, it would be her fault. Feeling the weight of her work, she bit her lip. She needed to begin the suitability inspection. "The day isn't getting any younger. How far is the drive to your home?"

"Two hours, give or take a few minutes." He nodded toward the window. "Light's fading fast, so if we're headed to the farm, we better get going." Jack motioned at the luggage next to Alice. "Let me load up yours and Charlotte's bags."

She hesitated for a moment and stood, trying to not wring her hands with worry. He had mentioned more than one bedroom. They'd have chaperones for her spending the night with him. Alice nodded, ignoring the pull of doubt. "We can manage, thank you." She smiled at the Hayses. "Children, I suppose you've eavesdropped on everything?"

Charlotte shook her head while the boys nodded. The girl looked from one adult to the other. "I tried not to, but wanted to know what would happen to us.

"I don't blame you a bit." Jack scooped up the children's bags with one hand. "Let's go home."

A taste of panic hit the back of her throat. He couldn't mean to settle them in as a single man. This farm visit wouldn't decide anything until she said so. Alice cleared her throat and said, "For now," while following him to the exit. "None of us can become too complacent until the adoption committee is consulted."

CHAPTER 4

THE STUFFING TAKEN OUT OF HIM, JACK'S SHOULDERS slumped like his mood. Not until she'd been so eager to separate the children had he realized how much he cared for them. He put the travel bags in the back. "Here. There's not a lot of room in the buggy. Get situated, and I'll find a better place for these."

He waited until Alice stepped up after Charlotte. Jack lifted his hand to scratch the back of his neck. He hadn't thought of all five of them on the wagon's bench. The day was too cold for the youngsters to ride in the back without cover. He couldn't help it now and said, "Might have to be cozy for a little while." The ladies sat close as the boys fought over who would get to perch on Alice's lap. He chuckled at the arguing. "Good thing we don't have a full day's drive," he said while hoisting himself up to the seat.

"A very good thing," Alice replied as Conner squirmed to get comfortable. She put the blanket over their laps, giving Jack his edge. "Here you are, and Conner, settle down, please."

"Ready?" he asked and clicked at Shep to start pulling. Each movement along the rough ground brushed the side of her thigh into his. Jack looked at her. With her head turned to Charlotte and Carter, she didn't notice him staring at her exposed neck. He took a deep breath; her smooth skin and rose fragrance teased him.

He sighed. Ellie might have been gone a few weeks, but they'd been fighting and distant for far longer. Most likely any woman would appeal to him at the moment. He gave her a side glance. Except this woman was even prettier up close. No, she didn't seem like just any ol' gal to him. Her body heat radiated toward his despite the layers they wore.

Jack shifted to ease away from Alice and respect her space but couldn't budge. She looked at him, and he gave her a slight smile. "Sorry."

"Don't be. If not for Conner I'd be cold and fidgeting, too." She lifted her chin toward the west. "We will get there before it's too dark, won't we?"

"Most likely." He snapped the reins with a pop. "Come on, Shep, we have places to be."

Alice put a hand on his upper arm. "Oh no, don't be mean to him." Her touch lingered as she added, "He's fine, really."

The squeeze she gave his bicep went through Jack, leaving his mouth dry and heart racing. "Yes, ma'am." When she smiled, letting her fingertips slide from him with a blush, he added, "But if he doesn't get a move on, we'll be feeling our way in the dark."

"Dark?" Charlotte said, her voice wavering.

Conner looked to Carter before adding, "We don't like the dark."

The four of them stared at him with wide eyes, and he laughed. "We'll be fine." He clicked a couple more times to the horse. "Still, hurrying a little couldn't hurt."

"Good," Alice said. She gave him a slight smile before staring ahead. "I don't care for pitch black."

Jack tilted his head, searching her expression. Her voice had wavered, hinting at a much deeper fear than her words portrayed. "Don't worry, Miss Alice. Not a lot happens around here. We're pretty civilized."

"Do you live in a sod house, Mr. Dryden?" Carter asked.

Conner added, "We learned about settlers baking mud into bricks at school."

He grinned at the thought of his refined wife tolerating a sod home for more than a year or two and shook his head. "Not anymore. We lived in a dugout for about a year. I built the house around it and turned the space into a root cellar."

Charlotte leaned forward and asked, "Is that like a basement?"

Remembering how a dugout home was odd to him at first, Jack nodded. They wouldn't have ever seen something built out of mud and grass in their young lives unless the train went farther west. "A lot like it, yes. The walls aren't brick or mason, yet."

"Yet?" Alice countered. "Do you have plans to expand the cellar into something more?"

Conner shook Jack's arm. "Like a dungeon? Can we help?"

He laughed at his simple room changing into an underground prison. Jack checked Alice's face to gauge her mood. Her expression stayed neutral, and the children seemed interested, so he replied, "I'm counting on it. A farm needs a lot of help to run well." He smiled, taking the chance to tell them more about the homestead. "I have cattle, horses—I mean a horse, Shep here, chickens, and an ox named Jimmy for heavy loads and farm work."

Carter asked, "What are the cows' names?"

"And the chickens?" Conner added.

"Haven't named them, yet." He glanced at Alice for confirmation. "I might leave all that to you four."

She frowned at him before saying, "I suppose letting us help you during our visit couldn't hurt."

Her reminder that the adoption wasn't a done deal sent a tremor through him. Jack frowned. He'd already grown used to the idea of the Hayses being Drydens someday soon. "Sure. And there might be some other small tasks they could help do, too."

The two boys began bouncing on the ladies' laps and cheering. "Stop moving around," Charlotte whined, each word louder than the last. "Your bony behind is hurting me."

"Boys, go to the back if you want to roughhouse." The two did as she suggested, jostling the adults and adolescent in their efforts.

Alice leaned closer to him. "You might be disappointed in those two farming. They've had more school time than field hand training."

Jack chuckled. If she thought to dissuade him from getting his hopes up about the children's capabilities, she'd already lost the battle. "I'm glad. Part of the conditions was to send them to school, wasn't it?" he asked, and Alice nodded. "Good, because the teacher is expecting all three of them."

She gasped. "You've spoken to him already?"

"Yes." He stared ahead, jaw set. Jack didn't want to see any disapproval in her face from him taking the initiative for his children. "When Sister Teresa sent the letter saying to expect you, I talked to Mr. Anders personally."

"I'm very pleased you care for them so much." She took hold of his bicep again. "Your doing so will help your argument to the agent." Alice gave his arm a squeeze before letting go of him.

A man could get used to affections from a pretty woman like her. He grinned. "Me, too, ma'am, and I'm willing to do whatever it takes to adopt."

"I'm hungry," Carter chimed in, pressing his face between Jack and Alice. "Will we have supper at your house, Mr. Dryden?"

"And water? Miss Alice never gave us food or water," Conner added from the back.

Jack grinned at Alice's gasp. "Now, I find that hard to believe about our dear Miss McCarthy."

Charlotte cleared her throat. "I'm thirsty, too, but they're exaggerating. We had lunch together."

"Children, please. We'll have a picnic at Mr. Dryden's house." She looked over at him with a hopeful smile.

He nodded while mentally going over his food stores. "I could rustle up some dinner for us all."

"I could cook if you like," Charlotte offered. "The sisters had us bigger girls learn how to keep house."

Jack looked to Alice for permission before replying, "Well, then. I'd like whatever you'd be able to cook."

"Thank you, Mr. Dryden," the girl said.

The appreciation shining in her eyes left him a little shy and a bit unsure of what else to say. He wasn't her pa yet, and besides, he didn't feel up to being the hero her expression made him out to be. Did every father have doubts? He'd have to ask his friend and the local adoption agent, Harry Donovan, to know for sure.

He didn't want to dwell on the negative until he had to do so. Plus, their confusion over what a root cellar was had him thinking they needed more details on farm life with him. Jack turned to Alice. "I think you and the children will enjoy my homestead."

Alice smiled. "I agree I will. Fresh air, blue skies, and people only when you want to see them." She breathed in deep. "Every time I return to the city, the air seems more intolerable. A person grows more accustomed to wildflowers far more than they ever do to sewage."

Jack chuckled. "I'd reckon so, ma'am. Ellie and I read about the horrible conditions for children back east. It's why I wanted to adopt."

She looked at him, eyebrows raised at first. "Thank you for your generosity. I wish more people felt as you do. It's been easier to find good homes for older children if they're well behaved and not ill." Alice indicated Conner with a nod of her head. "Healthy children are the easiest to place."

He glanced at Carter first and then Charlotte. The girl stared down while smoothing her dress from dust. Had one of them been ill, or was sick now and hiding it from him? They all seemed strong. Turning the family away just because one of them wasn't well seemed cruel and he smiled at Alice in reassurance. "I'm sure. A sickly child is a sad thing and something most people don't make time for healing. Scratching out a living on the frontier tends to cull the weak."

"Hmm. In my experience, the city leaves abandoned children little choice but to seek healthier climates." Alice stared ahead, jaw clenched. "The Hayses were all ill when the authorities brought them in to us." She put an arm around Charlotte. "All three are doing so well now and have nothing to worry about in finding a new home."

He gave both ladies a smile to reassure Charlotte and reached back to ruffle Conner's hair. "I agree. They seem in fine shape. The sisters have treated them very well."

One boy said, "I'm cold."

"Me too," the second added.

"Come on, then," Alice said, and the two boys returned to their places under the blanket.

"Now your behind is bony and cold," Charlotte said as Carter nestled into her warmth.

When they crested a hill, Jack could see the buildings of his farm. The low light barely hid them, and he decided to wait until pointing out their new home. He clicked to Shep, wanting to pick up the pace. "I didn't know the police brought them to the orphanage, though."

Charlotte said, "They did after I went to the station house. I was scared at first to tell anyone about Pa, but he wouldn't wake up."

Seeing the world through her eyes left a lump in Jack's throat. He never knew his father. Jack Sr. had died in the War Between the States when Jack was a baby. "You did the right thing in letting an adult know."

"Pa had always told us to keep to ourselves, don't steal, and always say we had a home even if we had to lie." She held on to her brother when the buggy hit a bump. "The boys sold newspapers, and I took care of our pa while he was sick. When he passed, the three of us didn't know what to do."

Alice put an arm around the girl. "Mr. Dryden is correct. You did the best thing possible and now have the chance for new parents and a new life."

She sniffed. "I know and thank you, Miss Alice." Charlotte gave Jack a slight smile. "Healthy parents are as important as healthy children."

He glanced at Charlotte and the boys. All three had the same profile. Jack had never awoken one morning and found one of his family members dead. He'd never been left alone in the world with a couple of siblings who might be taken from him by well-meaning adults. These children needed a stable home, a guardian they could count on, and Jack felt as if his only choice was to be their parent. "I agree with you and can promise I'm not going anywhere."

He turned onto the long driveway, the barren trees forming a lacy canopy over them in the last of the twilight. "Welcome home..." he began and, noticing Alice's silent warning frown, he added, "To my homestead, I mean."

"Can we race to the front door?" Carter asked.

Seeing Conner nod in agreement, Jack grinned and pulled Shep to a stop. "Go ahead." The two were on the ground before the buggy's wheels stopped rolling. "I'm glad there's just enough light to keep them out of trouble."

"Oh, they can run into a mess even at high noon, Mr. Dryden." Charlotte smiled at him. "If I weren't such a lady now, I'd beat the both of them to the house."

Alice chuckled. "If I weren't either, I'd be leading the way."

He grinned at the thought of the two city women racing to his front door. Jack glanced at Alice and corrected himself. Charlotte was a charming girl, not a woman, and not like her lovely guardian. "I'll ride up to the barn, unhitch Shep, and show you around while there's a bit of light left."

"I'd like that, thank you," Alice replied.

He nodded and looked out over his homestead. The place seemed smaller now that Jack looked through a stranger's point of view. He pulled the horse to a stop in front of the barn. This building was larger than his home, but then he'd had the neighbors help in building the barn, too.

Jack hopped down, extending a hand to help the women. When Alice accepted his offer, her firm grip on his hand hinted at the strength under her ladylike exterior. He'd managed to block out their touching during the wagon ride home, but now? This contact hit him like a mule's kick.

"Thank you," Alice murmured, the second word a little breathless with her landing.

The buggy squeaked as Charlotte sidled over, distracting him from watching Alice walk away. He refocused on the young girl as she held her hand out to him. Jack helped her to the ground, too. She was such a lovely young lady. "Careful, it's a ways down."

"Thank you, Mr. Dryden."

His wife should have stayed. Ellie was a fool to run away from a daughter like Charlotte, even if she didn't know it. He returned her grin. "You're welcome."

Both boys ran up to him, and Conner panted, "I won."

"This time," Carter hollered and tapped Jack before sprinting back to the house.

"Boys, stop," he hollered. When both halted and turned to him, Jack nodded towards the house. "There's a trail down to the creek. Race down the path, and halfway you'll find the chicken coop and smokehouse."

"Not race," Alice said. "Be careful."

"We'll have eggs for breakfast," Charlotte said.

"Good idea." He reached in for his guests' luggage. "Miss McCarthy, if you'll take these while I care for Shep?"

"Certainly," she said and added, "thank you" while taking the bags from him. Alice looked from him to the house and back. "Will we have a bedroom?"

"Sure, we do," he said without thinking, and she blushed. His face burned, too, at the sudden way his imagination leaped to them sharing a bed. Jack grinned, giving a mental shake to resume being mannerly. "I mean, you and Charlotte will share one while the boys and I will share the other."

"Thank you." She turned to the young girl. "Let's find you a bucket for the eggs, and I'll unpack for you three."

The two walked away, and Jack watched them for a couple of seconds before turning to Shep. "Come on, boy. Let's get you settled in for the night."

He led the horse and buggy to the barn. The day had been the exact opposite from what he'd expected when hitching up the horse for town. He undid the fastenings and led Shep to his stall. Instead of riding in, declining the adoption, and signing—

Jack halted, and Shep bumped into him. He'd forgotten the divorce papers entirely. Meeting the Hayses and Alice not only distracted him, but they'd thrown his entire day, if not life, off course. Ellie had been the love of his life. They'd meant to move west, start an empire of their own, complete with a large family. One by one, those dreams ended for them both. The only thing he had left was his small farm. Jack hovered between hope and despair, depending on what Alice and Donovan decided.

He eased the bit and halter from Shep's head, scratching behind the horse's ears with his free hand. "Alice," he said for only him and the animal to hear. She'd upset his plans even now. Her home was in a city he'd most likely never visit, and all he wanted was to learn everything about her. Jack never even considered finding another wife, but when Alice smiled at him with a twinkle in her eyes? He was smitten.

After shaking himself out of the daydream, he refreshed Shep's hay. With a parting pat to the horse's neck, he headed over to his three ladies. Each cow was heavy with calf and needed names from the Hays children. He grinned while adding hay to their trough. Jack looked forward to hearing what they'd come up with to call each animal. Satisfied the livestock had enough to eat and drink, he went back into the chilly evening. The wind picked up, spurring him into a brisk walk.

Once inside, the women's voices and doors creaking open and closed in the other rooms pleased him. The place had felt less like a home and more like a vacant house in the past week or so. He closed the door behind him, shrugging out of his jacket and hanging it up along with his hat. A row of coats was on the hooks to the right of his, and Jack almost chuckled at his plan working. He'd put them in right after receiving word about the children due to arrive.

"Hello," Alice said as she walked into the room. "The boys are still outside. Charlotte left to visit the henhouse just now, and I'd wanted to start a fire."

"No need to mess up your nice dress." As he spoke, Jack went over to the small woodpile. "I'll get something burning soon."

"I did check for an apron, thinking Mrs. Dryden might have left one behind."

He put kindling on the stacked wood inside the stove. "She didn't leave behind anything of hers. Even took one of the horses."

"That's a shame. Shep will get lonely without a companion."

He paused, the match he was about to strike hovering in mid-air. "Oh?" He continued with the motion, igniting the thin branches. "She was probably thinking of the journey home more than how the rest of us would feel." Jack paused at the slip before clearing his throat. Best to just ignore the slight confession and hope Alice didn't catch the resentment he felt toward Ellie.

"I expect so." She watched as he stood, his muscles a little stiff from the cold. "Your wife has been gone a month?"

"Yes, about that long." Now, since she'd asked, Jack wasn't sure of the exact length of time. He walked over to his coat and pulled the divorce and adoption envelopes from his pocket. He gave the decree another read-through. The document looked harmless enough. The first time he'd read it, the first few words had broken his heart and almost his spirit, too. But now while reviewing them? The pain didn't seem real right now. "It's been a month and a day."

"I'm sorry."

Her sympathy broke through his musings. Jack glanced up at her and tried to give her a reassuring smile. "Thank you. So am I. I loved her and expected our vows to last far longer than they did."

"Do you think she'll return someday?"

He folded the papers before laying them on the table. "That's an excellent question." Jack picked up the adoption information's envelope, tapping the edge against his hand. He wanted to be honest and say Ellie was never coming back. The paper hitting his palm tapped out in the silence, broken only by the firewood popping. If he told the truth, would Alice allow him to adopt the children? Probably not. He had to keep her from refusing him outright. "I think—"

CHAPTER 5

THE BACK DOOR BUSTING OPEN INTERRUPTED HIM.
"We found the chicken coop!" Carter shouted.

Conner jostled his brother as the two ran up to the adults.
"You should have seen them. The big one tried to kill me."

The twins spoke over each other about their poultry
encounter until Jack held up a hand. "What about your
sister?"

"She saved us from the big chicken," Carter said. "She
waved him back, so we could escape."

"Saved our lives," Conner added. "We would have died."

Jack glanced at Alice and shared a look. They both were on
the same page, especially with her biting her lip to not
laugh outright. "I'd better go make sure she's unharmed. I'll

send her to the house but might be a while myself since I have animals to feed, eggs to gather, and water to carry." He went for his coat, still drying on its peg.

"Wait a moment." Alice took his arm. "Could the boys help you do chores and see what farm work is like?"

He put a hand over hers. They remained in contact for a few moments until she slipped away from his touch. Her action broke him from their trance, and he grinned. "I figured they'd learn soon enough, but you're right. Why not? No time like the present." Jack turned to the boys. "Are you two ready?"

"Yeah," they both hollered, and Carter added, "Teach me how to wrangle that chicken."

"You bet." He went to get the water bucket and a pail for the eggs. "Maybe we can talk your sister into helping us."

The door opened, and Charlotte walked in while holding eggs close to her. "Look what I found. It was just like Sister Brigit said. Reach under while cooing at them and look."

Both boys reached for the eggs, their sister letting them take a few. Carter held one up to the lamplight. "This one is still warm."

"So is this one," Conner replied. "Feel."

The three of them swapped eggs back and forth, marveling over each one. Jack glanced over at Alice as she watched. She was a pretty woman in any light, but from the lamp? Her fair hair gleamed. He couldn't help but chuckle when curiosity won, and she reached out for a warm egg of her own to hold. "It's getting too dark out for all of us to be wandering around out there. I'll go and get water. There's bacon in the pantry cupboard. I cut extra at dinner last night for today."

Alice paused in examining the egg. "It is very pretty, Carter." She addressed Jack. "Are there morning chores we can help with tomorrow?"

"There are if you all don't sleep late enough to miss them."

"We won't," Charlotte said while putting the remaining eggs on the table. "I want to see more of the farm in the daylight."

"Good," Jack replied on his way to the back door. Nothing would be finished tonight if he kept hanging around in here, trying to keep from staring at Alice. "I'll be back in a bit."

He hurried outside. The air seemed to freeze in his throat, and he didn't want to take his time. The pump handle stuck to his skin. He muttered a muffled oath while retrieving a glove and resuming the actions. The bucket full, he paused for a moment. A less distracted man would have checked the coop, smokehouse, and barn for the night.

Jack grinned, not minding the full bucket while making his rounds. The children in his home and his finding Miss McCarthy attractive gave him hope for the future. He could be charming and persuasive when he wanted to be. All he had to do was give Donovan the facts, convince Alice the Hayses would thrive, and everything would be settled.

He stepped onto the back porch, stomping his feet free of extra snow at the same time. Stepping inside, Jack lifted his chin a little bit, realizing dinner smelled better than it had in a while. "I can tell you found the bacon."

The girl gave him a smile before turning back to her work. "I did. You'd mentioned the food cabinet, and I figured I had to check the containers around here."

Alice pressed her fingertips against her temples and said, "Tell me you didn't snoop."

The girl's smile fell as she wrung her hands. "Sorry, but I only looked for food and nothing else."

The fearful and worried expression on the young girl's face broke his heart. He had to reassure her. "It's all right. I want her and the boys to make themselves at home." He set the pail down by the stove and began removing his outerwear.

"Thank you, Mr. Dryden," Charlotte said before the bacon's pop distracted her. "I found some preserves, too." She strained to reach a higher shelf above the pantry.

"Here, let me help." He gave her the jam and retrieved the plates stacked just below it. Handing Charlotte a serving platter, too, he gave Alice the same smile he used on his mom to keep him out of trouble. "Once they have a chance to settle in, you'll see this is the perfect place for them."

She pursed her lips while taking the plates from him and setting the table. "I'll try to keep an open mind, but you know we're only staying tonight. Silverware?"

He frowned. "Yes, right here." Jack grabbed a jar full of cutlery and set it in the middle of the table. One night wasn't long enough. With the girl having learned how to cook and as full of energy as the boys were, they'd be just fine as a family. As long as he moved almost everything to within Charlotte's reach. He pulled out a kitchen chair for Alice. "You're welcome to spend the week here."

She sat, fussing with her skirts as she did so. "I can't without causing a delay at the main office."

Jack joined her at the table. Her use of "I" instead of "we" seemed encouraging. "I don't mind taking you to town, so you can send a telegraph to Sister Teresa." A grateful light flashed in her eyes. "Tomorrow, maybe the day after. Whenever you decide."

"I shouldn't put off returning home." She chewed on a part of her bottom lip for a few seconds before narrowing her eyes. "We could spend the day in town tomorrow while I talk to the various committee members about you caring for the children by yourself. Afterward, I can send a telegraph saying I'll be leaving here in three days."

Charlotte set the food down in front of the adults and went to the back door. "Boys? Dinner is ready."

Jack wanted to ask Alice to stay longer. He stood and brought up the extra chairs he'd made for them. Glancing at her soft brown hair gleaming in the firelight, a guilty twinge settled in his gut. He hadn't even signed the divorce papers, never mind filing them at the courthouse. They'd all be better off if Alice went home and Ellie came back to be the mother they'd both planned on her being.

After dragging the dining chairs in place, he rushed to set the table as the youngsters fought over who sat next to whom. Jack quieted the fuss by saying over them, "No need to argue about where you sit. We can change seats from one meal to the next."

The boys started shoveling food onto their plates. Charlotte did, too, he noticed, but a little more mannerly than her brothers. Jack tried to hide a smile and glanced over at Alice. She returned his grin with one of her own. He paused for a brief second before settling into his chair. The young woman's amusement contrasted so much with Ellie's unhappiness in the past several months.

Jack snuck another peek at her and caught the rosy glow of her cheeks in the soft light. She glanced over at him again as the twins argued. His face burned at her knowing expression. He straightened in his chair and refocused on his dinner. Any man would stare. Especially if a pretty gal like Alice sat beside him at the table.

"Mr. Dryden? Are you not hungry?" Charlotte asked. "I can cook something else if you'd rather."

He nodded at Charlotte, grateful to have his attention turned somewhere else. A weathervane stayed steadier in a thunderstorm than his thoughts did around her. He reached for what was left of the scrambled eggs. "These are perfect; keep on eating your dinner." Jack dropped the scoop onto his plate and didn't let the bacon leave his hand before taking a bite.

Alice added, "I agree. You've outdone anyone else's food I've ever tried."

Charlotte smiled down at her plate. "I just fixed them the way Sister Brigit taught me, us. That's all. I'm sure farm girls cook eggs out here all the time."

"I suppose they do, but still." Alice held up a forkful. "You'll be an excellent blend of town and country by the time you're grown."

Jack pushed his empty plate forward. He'd have plenty of time to learn more about the girl he wanted to be his daughter. Alice, on the other hand, would be gone in less than a week. Against his better judgment, he wanted to know more about her before she left. "What about you? Are you a farm or city girl?"

"City. New York, to be exact," she replied while clearing the table. "I never stepped foot outside of the state until earlier this year." Alice gave the younger girl their dishes.

"We're from the same place," Carter said, and Conner nodded. "But our mother and father wasn't."

"Weren't," Charlotte corrected on her way to the wood stove.

"Yeah, they wasn't."

Jack nodded, trying to hide a grin lest they thought he was laughing at them. The boys had wolfed down their food without talking. Charlotte did the same, only with far more manners. And Alice? He'd noticed she took small bites as if to make the meal last longer, or to maybe savor every crumb. Either way, Jack found her interesting.

The four of them looked bone-tired, and he stood. "I usually wash up before breakfast. Set the frying pan out back, and the possums will clean it up for us by the morning."

First one boy, then the other began laughing until Conner said, "Possums don't do dishes."

"They do out here, cleaning up with a couple of licks or two." Jack winked at the boys and nodded toward the disgust on the ladies' faces. "I might be joshing you all, too."

Charlotte sighed. "Oh, thank goodness. If possum spit was a normal occurrence, I'd be going home with Miss Alice."

Jack shook his head, chuckling. "No, I don't employ any critters to do my clean-up. It's just me and...um, me." He glanced at Alice as she went to the back door and said to the others, "I'd rather have your help in dishwashing than any ol' varmint's."

"I can lick plates just fine," Carter offered.

Charlotte gave the table a final wipe as Conner put the last chair in place. "He can, but I'd rather use your washtub." When Jack chuckled, she sighed. "I'm glad no one around here has to clean anything with his tongue. Yuck."

"I agree," Alice said as she stepped up and made shooing motions toward the three of them. "Come on, time for bed." She led them toward the bedrooms. "Do you need help with your prayers tonight?"

The children shook their heads, adding a mumbled "No, ma'am," as they followed her.

He looked around the cabin with fresh eyes, seeing the place from his guests' point of view. Nice house, could use some cleaning in the corners. Not a bad home and had a solid floor. He smiled at the memory of walking into the finished house for the first time. Fresh new wood, curtains ready for windows, and only one bedroom for him and Ellie.

"I hope you don't mind."

He turned in the chair to find Alice with her journal in hand. Jack had been lost in his own thoughts and guessed she wanted to sit with him. He hoped so, anyway. "No, not at all." As she settled in, he asked, "Do you need a pen and ink?" He stood. "I have both handy."

She smiled. "Thank you for the offer, but no. I have a pencil."

"They make things easier, don't they?" He went to the cupboard. "We, or I, tend to use ink exclusively, but like being able to erase my mistakes instead of starting over with a fresh sheet of paper."

She watched as he placed the inkwell, pen, and farm journal on the table. As he sat down again, Alice said, "Now that you mention it, a fresh start with anything sounds lovely."

Despite the temptation to do so, he didn't glance at her writing. He kept his eyes on his own work to respect her privacy and said, "I'd agree with you on most things in life, but the same document several times? I don't need so much penmanship practice, ever."

Alice laughed before putting a hand over her mouth. "Goodness! Now I'm glad I use a pencil most of the time. Not that I never use ink. I do, when the occasion calls for it."

"Legal papers," he offered, the divorce nudging at the edge of his mind. The pull he felt toward her surged stronger. With the Hayses becoming his children, she might have a reason to visit while on her way to placing other orphans. "Those and bank papers if need be." He smiled. "Everything else is pencil so I can make corrections."

Alice chuckled, returning his smile. "Exactly. I never use pencil on adoption papers."

She'd opened the door for him, and he wanted to jump through with both feet. Setting his pen down, he asked, "About that. How likely is it you'll need my pen for the Hays children's adoption?"

CHAPTER 6

Jack wanted to reach out and grab the words before they reached her ears. More so when she frowned. After a couple of seconds, Alice cleared her throat while slowly closing her journal with the pencil inside to mark the place.

"I can't make a solid promise but do think there's an excellent chance they'll be placed with you." She stared at the lantern in the middle of the table with her hands folded in her lap. "I must be frank. Having Mrs. Dryden here would have helped your case, of course."

He'd known better than to ask outright and so soon. Unable to help himself, he asked, "There's nothing more I could do?"

"Not at the moment." She looked up at him, tilting her head. "You seem to have provided a more than adequate home with plenty of opportunities for them to gain real skills and schooling. Provided I get good references from the committee despite your lack of a wife, I'd say there a possibility you'll run out of signing ink soon."

Her words gave his heart permission to do more than hope, and Jack grinned. He'd take any chance he could get no matter how slim. "Great. I'm glad to hear it." He stared unseeing at his farm accounts. The instant family meant he'd be able to keep the homestead and provide a good life for the children. All the plans he'd dreamed back when starting the process now seemed a lot more possible, and he sighed in relief. "I've been a lot more worried than I thought I'd be, I guess."

"Most people are. Even those with finalized adoptions somehow can't believe their good luck. I receive thank-you letters quite often in this work."

He glanced at Alice to find her looking at him with a slight smile. "I reckon you do." Her cheeks flushed, and she lowered her chin. He leaned forward, resting an elbow on the table. "What happens after you leave the children with me?"

She bit her lip for a second before replying, "After our orphans are placed, someone will do welfare checks on them. Routine, and merely for everyone's benefit."

"Of course." He grinned at her coming back to Liberty regularly. Before he could change his mind, Jack asked, "How long will your visits here be? Should I build another bedroom for you just in case you need to stay for a while? I don't mind."

Alice's jaw dropped for a moment. "I, uh, no." She shook her head. "No need to trouble yourself, Mr. Dryden." She shook her head. "Truly. Any visits will be brief and most likely not done by me."

Her face glowed dusky pink in the lamplight. Her embarrassment, while adorable, seemed odd to Jack. If he worked at the Home, he'd have to follow up just to satisfy his curiosity. "And you've never considered stopping by on a train trip farther west to visit any of the families you've approved?"

Clearing her throat, she reached for her book and held it up against her chest like a shield. "Oh, you mean for a brief— well, I've never had the opportunity although I've written several letters to the older children. The ones who could read. Because they could. So, I did." Alice took a deep breath. "I mean, I've never had my own bedroom and wouldn't know what to do with so much space."

He smiled at her fluster. The color never faded from her face, reminding him of how much younger she must be than he was. "Then I'll be sure to build you a room of your own. If you could come to visit and stay here for more than a day or two, I'd like to be prepared."

Her eyes met his, deep blue in the lamplight. "You're kind, but there's no need to do anything of the sort. The Home will make hotel provisions for all of its agents, no matter who visits you."

"I had hoped you'd be our only agent," he said, his voice huskier than he expected it to be.

Her eyebrows rose, and a slight smile played about her lips. "I see. Well, we have many people in our organization who place orphans. I'm not the only one and can't visit every family. You might be disappointed."

"Yeah, you're right. I meant the agent. Ours. All of us," Jack stammered. In a desperate bid to change the subject from her being exclusive to his new family, he cleared his throat and asked, "Miss McCarthy, do you have more children to escort soon after this adoption?"

She relaxed, placing her journal on the table. "Yes. There are many more babies and youngsters who need good homes. I'll need to hurry back to the Home and help with the next group."

He missed her already, and they'd only met a few hours ago. In an effort to learn more about Alice in the short time they had left, Jack wanted to find a reason for her to stop in Liberty again in the near future. Ignoring their fatigue he pressed on, asking her, "How many trips west have you been on so far?"

Alice focused on her book, opening it to the place held by her pencil. "One this far, but several more back east."

Jack fidgeted in his chair, the rope seat squeaking against the wood frame. He had to know if she enjoyed traveling west, maybe planned on living here one day. "Did you want to venture farther, or were the Hayses an exception?"

"I'd like to, maybe. When the Home mentioned this placement, I volunteered to be the caretaker because of the location." Alice wrote the month and year in her book before glancing up at him with a smile. "A sister came to our orphanage when I was ten or eleven, telling us all about her life in the wilderness." Her words slow at first as she turned back to her journal, she said, "Sister... I can't even remember her name now, had lost her family, too, and decided to help others from then on. After that, the west had always seemed like a place where kind people lived." She gave him a quick glance before retracing the date. "I'd always wanted to see for myself."

Alice's dream registered in his mind, but her lack of anyone in the world except the nuns stuck the most. He'd left his extended family with the certainty they'd always be there if he wanted to return or send for them. "You have no family at all?"

She drew a square below the date on her page, not looking up at him. "No. My mother left me with the nuns when I was a baby. Nothing but my name on a scrap of paper." She shook her head. "I don't remember her or my father."

Her words embedded themselves into his heart as if hammer-driven. To be so alone with no kin seemed impossible to Jack. No wonder she seemed reluctant to talk about herself. "I'm sorry."

"Thank you. It happened, and I survived." Alice looked up at him with a strained smile. "Now I help other children. Simple as that."

Watching her draw small houses out of the squares she'd made under the date, he smiled. Did she plan on sketching a full scene instead of writing anything? Jack wanted to give her a bigger piece of paper and plenty of pencils. So, Alice was kind-hearted as well as artistic. He wondered if the Home would be her life's work and if she ever planned on following a calling. Before thinking, he asked, "Do you plan on becoming a sister, too?"

"Maybe." Alice glanced at him, a blush creeping across her face. "Probably not, since I've heard from every one of them that it's a passion to a higher purpose." She began doodling opposite from the dated page. "I haven't felt the need, myself, so I assist in other ways."

He watched, fascinated, as a tree took shape on the paper. Jack couldn't look away from the landscape unfolding under her pencil. "One of my cousins who is a minister says the same is true for him. He and his wife both believe no other way of life is for them."

She smiled, not pausing in her sketch. "Do they live here in Missouri?"

"No, back in Kentucky." He hesitated a second before adding, "Ellie and I came west after the war, wanting a fresh start to our new lives." Somehow, bringing his absent and soon-to-be former wife into the conversation seemed wrong to Jack. He wanted to focus on Alice for as long as she was here.

"Pardon my saying so, but you don't seem old enough to have fought in the war. Not even as a boy lying about his age."

He chuckled, glad to have avoided the whole Ellie topic. Maybe his ego was a little pleased Alice considered him younger than his father, too. Unless she happened to like older men, and then he was... Jack shook himself. None of that mattered until he signed the divorce and he replied, "Thank you. I'm not at all. We came here in '74."

"That's a long time after the war. Did any of your slaves stay despite emancipation?"

He stifled a sigh. It seemed every big-city Northerner thought every small-town Southerner had slaves. "We didn't own anyone, and the war's effects never seemed to end. The Dryden farm was a small patch of land my brother was going to work after he returned from the army." Jack gave a slight smile as she sketched the Liberty train depot next to her tree. There really wasn't a tree nearby, but he liked the idea of a shady place for passengers to rest so much he couldn't correct her. "Our family couldn't afford much, including purchasing another person, so we did everything ourselves."

Alice gave him an intense stare. "You left nearly a decade after the war ended. Would your brother not share the land with you?"

Jack straightened in his chair, unwilling to talk about the events in anything but a matter-of-fact way. To do anything else hurt too much to bear. "He would have, but he didn't return from the battlefield." He ran a hand through his hair, wanting to be unaffected, but not sure how to be. "First my mother grew sick and died, then my father. I tried to keep the place going, but the property taxes and new fees ate up everything. I had to sell."

"Hmm." Alice interlaced her fingers, staring into the lamplight. "I don't suppose Mrs. Dryden is waiting for you there, then."

He scratched the back of his neck. "No. She's not waiting anywhere but at her parents' home in Boston." Jack looked over at Alice to find her staring at him, curiosity clearly etched on her face. "I'd made a mistake marrying a Yankee from Massachusetts, I suppose. She was, is, pretty, kind, and well-to-do.

"So why did she marry me and come out west, you ask?" Jack stood and went to the high shelf above the stove. He retrieved a small flask of whiskey, half full, and a small glass next to it. He blew out the dust and went to his chair.

"Right now, I don't have an answer for you because she's not here to tell me why, either."

He poured a finger's width of liquor into the glass. "Ellie loved me, I suppose, and the homestead was our grand adventure together. I'd warned her before we left Kentucky about how all this would take work and she agreed to everything." He lifted the bottle. "Want to share?"

She waved her hand while closing her journal. "No. I've promised to never touch a drop. The nuns discouraged me from becoming too western and wild out here."

"Mighty wise of them." Jack chuckled at the description, her concerned expression and kind eyes warming his heart. He wanted to ask if the frontier's reputation was the reason for her visit more than the kindness of strangers. He figured he knew which answer she'd give but decided to let the matter sleep for a while.

At some point, he supposed, a man would want more than sympathy from such a lovely young lady. But right now, Jack was fine with what he could have from her. "I reckon a woman can't be too careful." He drank the whiskey in one gulp, the burning trail the liquid left matching the ache in his heart. "A bottle a year and the rare drink at the saloon are about as wild as I get."

She gave him a wry smile. "Everyone needs a little vice in their lives, or there'd be nothing for Father O'Brien to listen to during confessional. Speaking of doing things we'll later regret," Alice picked up her journal and said, "it's late, and you've given me a lot to think about concerning the Hays children's futures here."

He stared at the empty glass, worried. Had the small drink been wrong? Too bad for an adoption agent to overlook? He'd vow to never touch the stuff again if it kept the children here. "Some of it good, I hope?"

"Some, yes." She took a few steps toward the bedroom before turning toward him. "I look forward to talking more with you tomorrow."

"As do I. Goodnight, Miss McCarthy."

"Goodnight, Mr. Dryden."

He watched until she disappeared into the darkened bedroom. Left alone with his feelings, he didn't know what to untangle first. His attraction for Alice resulting in his betrayal of Ellie's memory? He snorted. The woman hadn't died, just ran off. He stood, taking the glass and whiskey with him. His fascination with a young lady didn't surprise him. She was pretty, and he was a man. Simple as that.

Jack put the items back where they belonged on the high shelf and walked to his bedroom, treading lightly in his boots so as not to wake the others. As he crept into the room, he eased to the side of the bed and undressed down to his underclothes.

After he slipped in under the covers and was alone with his thoughts as one of the boy's soft snoring would let him be, Jack searched his feelings about tonight's chat. He'd learned so much about Alice yet wanted to know more. As he turned to his side, away from the boys, Jack wondered. Would he be as fascinated with her if Ellie had stayed? He closed his eyes. Maybe? Yes? No? He didn't know anything for sure anymore. Not since he'd watched Ellie leave and after bringing Alice here.

CHAPTER 7

ALICE FELT HER WAY ALONG THE BED'S EDGE IN Charlotte's room, careful to not wake her. The slight breaths from the sleeping girl encouraged her to stay quiet. She found her carpetbag on the floor at the side and knelt, opening it by touch.

She searched for and pulled out her nightgown. Worried about being caught while undressing, Alice looked toward the doorway. The wood stove's scant light illuminated the main living area. Jack wouldn't be able to see her undress here in the darkness. She undid the buttons down the front of her garment, some popping free easier than others. Working fast in the cool air, she pulled off her clothes and quickly put on her worn nightgown.

The light from the doorway dimmed to nearly nothing, and she froze. The floor creaked as he went to his own bedroom. She listened for but didn't hear a pause in his footsteps. The house quieted, and she started breathing again.

She felt her way onto the bed and under the covers. The cold from the cotton sheet sank into her bones. Alice's body heat took a while to warm the surrounding blankets pressing down on her. In the cocoon of goose down, she stared into the unbroken darkness. If she listened carefully, she could hear Jack rustling around as he readied for sleep.

When the rope mesh of his and the boys' bed groaned with his weight, she let out her pent-up breath. His drinking had bothered her, but not for the reasons she was sure Jack expected. Alice closed her eyes and turned to her side. As he'd drunk liquor right in front of her tonight, all she'd wanted to do was taste the alcohol from his lips with her own.

No wonder the sisters discouraged young women her age from being agents so far west. If the bottle had been bigger than a pint and he'd approached her with the sweet, warm flavor on his lips? She nestled into the blankets. Sister Brigit would have strong words about Jack. Father O'Brien would offer to forgive him in confessional. And yet, Alice didn't feel as if Jack needed absolution. The man might drink, but it didn't make him a bum. Not by a long shot and not like others she'd seen in the bigger cities. Alice would rather think about his ready smile and general decency than dwell on anything bad about the man.

"Miss Alice?"

She smiled at Charlotte's sleepy and small voice. "Yes?"

"Will you let us stay with Mr. Dryden?"

Alice paused. The hope in the young girl's voice broke her heart. She didn't want to say no, yet saying yes right now was vastly premature. She turned over to face her and whispered, "I would like to, but need to interview his references in town first."

"Mr. Dryden is so much like Pa. It's as if he's come back to us."

She winced at the comparison between Dryden and the Hayses. All four of them, with herself included, had let their hopes rise too high. If Alice struggled with remembering to be impartial, the children had to have set their minds on Jack as their new pa. Giving in and letting the Hayses be adopted without a complete investigation went against every bit of her training. The sisters would be horrified, as would Father O'Brien.

Still, she needed to see the homestead for herself before taking the children back to the Home. They had to understand her motives. She wanted what was best for everyone and replied, "I'm sorry that I can't give you an answer now."

"Mm-hmm."

The bed moved a little as Charlotte shifted positions. Alice swallowed the lump in her throat, hoping her reasoning was good enough. A couple of shakes vibrated from the girl's side and then a few quiet sobs. "Charlotte, are you all right?"

"Yeah," she replied.

The shaking continued, and Alice knew the girl hadn't been honest. She put a hand on the girl's shoulder. "Please don't cry. Everything will be fine. You know what the sisters and Father O'Brien say."

"Uh-huh, but what if the committee refuses Mr. Dryden's request? What if the boys can stay here and I can't? What if someone mean adopts me and I have to stay with them forever?"

Alice gave Charlotte a reassuring squeeze. "I promise I'll do whatever I can to convince the men to let you three stay here and together." Her eyes adjusted to the low light, she smoothed the girl's hair from her face. "Mr. Dryden and his wife were approved once. Approving him a second time will be a formality, I'm sure."

"Do you really think so?" she asked with a sniff.

"Yes, I do."

She flopped over and snuggled closer to Alice, hugging her for a moment. "Thank you, Miss McCarthy."

"You're welcome." Alice smiled before realizing the room was too dark to see in. "Now try to get some sleep. We have a busy day tomorrow."

"Yes, ma'am." Charlotte turned over, facing away from Alice, and stirred under the covers for a few seconds.

Alice also turned away from the girl and closed her eyes. She didn't exactly bear false witness. Promising something to a child based on the actions of strangers worried her, though. She consciously relaxed her clenched fists. Either the adoption would proceed as planned, or the Hays children would be placed together with a new set of parents. Simple as that.

THE NEXT MORNING, THE SMELL OF COFFEE NUDGED Alice awake. She stirred, smiling and breathing in deep as if the aroma alone could fuel her. Voices drifted in, and she could pick out Jack and Charlotte's only. She opened her eyes, the soft light of dawn greeting her.

She sat up, swinging her legs onto the cold wooden floor. After a little shiver, she leaned forward to see if anyone would notice before hurrying out of her nightgown and into her dress. Buttoning up while turned away from the door, she looked out the window to see a cleared field surrounded by trees. Frost glittered in the sun's rays. Alice shook off the lovely distraction and quickly made her bed.

Wool socks helped but didn't keep her feet completely warm. She pulled on her shoes, and her chilled fingers fumbled a little. Eggs hissed in the frying pan, and Alice hurried toward the door to see if Charlotte needed help with breakfast.

The floor squeaked when she set foot outside of the bedroom. Morning light streamed in through the south windows, showing the dust in the air. Alice stared at Jack as he turned to face her.

He grinned. "Good morning, late bird. You must have been worn out from yesterday."

His reminder of the full day she'd had yesterday gave her the urge to yawn. She stifled the need and returned his smile with a glance toward Charlotte at the stove. "I suppose I was. Trains are both exhilaratingly fast and exhausting, it seems."

Jack stood and went for the cupboard. "I've got something that'll perk you right up."

She watched as he reached for a cup. "Not too strong, I hope."

"No, well, not to me." He poured coffee for her, setting the tin cup on the table in front of the chair she'd used last night. "Ellie always found it needed watering down." He paused for a moment before heading to the door. "I'll be right back."

His walking away gave Alice the chance to get up and go over to Charlotte. "Do you need help? Where are your brothers?"

"The boys are out causing trouble, I'm sure. I was paying more attention to starting breakfast than them." She slid the last egg onto the serving plate. "I must ask Mr. Dryden what I can use for dinner. He won't want eggs and bacon every meal."

"Ah." She set the table the same way Jack had done at dinner last night. "I'll call them in." Alice hurried to the back door just as Jack opened it. He stood in front of her, his face mirroring her surprise. Even up close, she found him very handsome. His eyes had a hint of dark circles his smile couldn't hide. Freezing air blew in as they stood there, gazes locked on each other. She shivered and murmured, "I should move," before stepping out of his way.

"I wouldn't mind coming inside where it's warm." He walked in, still grinning at her. "Especially when invited so nicely." Continuing to the table, he added, "I brought fresh water. Figured you might want some with the meal."

"Thank you." After a lingering glance at him, Alice stuck her head out the open doorway. "Boys, breakfast is ready," she hollered, her breath visible in the cold. A movement caught her eye as Conner and Carter topped a slight hill. They ran toward her, pants soaked to the knees. "What on earth happened?"

Conner reached her first as Carter trailed by a few inches, saying, "The ice isn't thick enough to slide on, and we fell through."

"Oh, for shame, both of you." She put her hands on her hips. "This won't do. We need to visit people in town and now look at you." Alice waved a hand at their feet. Dead leaves, tiny twigs, and clay mud clung to the sides of their shoes. "Your best clothes, too."

Charlotte behind her muttered, "Their only clothes, you mean."

Also behind her and on the other side, Jack chuckled. "I'll grab a couple of small blankets. You two stay there for a moment."

She frowned as he disappeared, then reappeared. "What did you want to do first?"

"Well." He brushed past her, putting a hand on her shoulder to steady as he went to his bedroom. "Find something of mine for them to wear," he hollered. "Then, get them out of the wet shoes, socks, and pants and have them eat breakfast while I hang up the wet things."

Alice bit her lip at the idea of Carter and Conner in the larger man's clothes. She glanced over at Charlotte, and when their gazes met, both women started laughing.

Jack reentered with what he'd found for them. After a glance at Alice, he grinned. "I expect it'll be funny until their clothes are dry." He unfolded a pair of pants and began rolling up the cuffs. "After taking the legs up a bit, either boy can wear this until noon."

"I can help hang up their clothes." Out of habit, Alice searched his walls for the clothesline. Not even a hint of a cord jutted out, and she realized no one in the country needed to keep clotheslines inside. "I'll be..." she said as the boys shut their bedroom door. "You all can hang everything out to dry, and they'll stay clean."

"You all hang your laundry inside?" he asked.

"Not everyone does," she said and walked to the window. "We're just particular about factory soot on our white collars."

"I can't blame you. Everything outside of town is cleaner." The floorboards creaked a bit as he went to stand behind her. "The fabric might be frozen stiff, but it'll be dry, don't worry."

She tried to focus on the sunny morning, but imagining his body heat so close kept her befuddled. His warm leather and coffee smell appealed to her as much as his way with words. If he'd been a single man, she might imagine a future with him.

Alice almost shook her head. She wouldn't be here at all without a Mrs. coupled with the Mr. Dryden to adopt the children. After a sigh, she said, "I spent a lot of time watching the land pass by us on the way here." She turned to find he stood a little too close, blocking her from seeing anything but him. His eyes reflected the window, his green turned turquoise from picking up the sky's hue. Her mouth went dry, and she whispered, "Maps say we're only a third of the way across the continent."

Jack looked at her, the corner of his eyes wrinkling when his gaze met hers. As quietly as she had said, he replied, "I've had family go to the Pacific and come back."

"I can't imagine even taking the chance to travel so far. Have you been?" she asked, and he shook his head. Alice continued, "You have to tell me everything that happened on their journey to and fro. I've only ever read newspaper reports."

He shrugged. "I don't know if I can. Might take me a week or so to tell you everything."

His humor didn't surprise her as much as the brief longing skirting across his face. Her breath caught. Jack couldn't feel this attraction she held for him, could he? And return her feelings? She dismissed the crazy notion and tried to smile through her surprise. "I might stay a little long—"

Charlotte cleared her throat. "I'll have to cook some more eggs. We were hungrier than I thought."

The adults broke off their conversation to check the table. Jack laughed at the empty serving plate while Alice frowned at the children's bad manners. Hunger was one thing. Eating the new parent out of house and home another, particularly when the food had smelled so good. She went around Jack to the stove. "Oh, dear. What have we discussed about behavior and sharing with others?"

"Don't mind them, miss," Jack began. She frowned at him, and his grin deepened. "I'll go back to the chicken coop and smokehouse."

She waited until he'd left the home before addressing the children. "Well?"

"We're sorry," the boys chanted in unison.

"And you, Charlotte?" she asked as the girl put her hands behind her and stared at the floor. "Is this how a lady acts?"

"No, ma'am."

Alice's stomach growled, echoing in the room. She glanced down at her abdomen, shocked at how loud her body had been. A snicker from first one boy then the other got her attention, and she scowled until Charlotte began giggling, too. "Fine. Yes, I'm angry because I'm hungry."

The door opened, and Jack came in, saying, "The ham could use a couple more days, but this hunk of belly is ready." All four of them began laughing, and he paused on his way to the stove. "Did I miss something?"

Conner nudged Carter, who said, "Miss McCarthy's belly was talking to us."

"My stomach growled," she added as he handed the food to Charlotte. Alice smiled at the girl. "I can cook our breakfast."

"So can I." She added coffee into both adult's cups. "Here. I've warmed this a little for the wait."

"Perfect." Jack winked at the boys. "Want to help me show Miss McCarthy our farm?"

Carter jumped up, catching the chair before it fell backward. "Yeah!"

"She can see where we fell through the ice." Conner hollered while running around the table to their wet coats. He tossed one to his brother. "We'll show you."

"I don't trust you two yet, and you'll show her the hole after everything is dried." Jack ruffled Conner's hair. "Hang your clothes over the railing, and I'll check on them in a while." He took a sip before adding, "Miss McCarthy, bring your coffee and coat. You'll want both once outside."

She enjoyed seeing the children minding Jack so well and wondered how long the good behavior would last. Alice went to where her outerwear hung on its peg and began putting on her coat. "Does laundry take quite a while to dry out west?" She struggled to reach behind for her sleeve. "Some days, my stockings stay damp for hours."

"Here, let me help you." Jack held up her coat for her arm, and she slid into the chilly fabric. "Depends on what time of year. Winter is faster, but I wasn't teasing. Fabric can get board-stiff when it's freezing."

She laughed, imagining her skirts on a frosty laundry day. "I wouldn't need hoops for my dress, then."

His face a little red, he said, "No, I suppose not. Spring and summer are a lot more humid around here. Here in the draw, we don't get a lot of wind, either." Jack grabbed his coat and began putting it on. "Do you have gloves?" he asked, and she nodded. "Good, you'll need them. A trip to the henhouse is one thing. Showing a pretty lady around the homestead might take longer."

Her cheeks burned as she fished in her pocket for her cotton gloves and pulled them on. She was probably being shy for nothing, but still. He'd used "pretty" to describe her, and Alice wasn't sure if he was serious. "I don't know about my appearance." Her hand shook with a slight tremor as she reached for her coffee cup and took a sip. "I always strive for functional and decent."

He held the door open for her as she walked through. "You do quite well in everything, ma'am," and said to Charlotte, "We won't be long. I'm not giving my breakfast another chance to disappear."

Alice walked down the wooden steps, marveling at the frosty landscape in front of her. Trees on the north side of the house kept her from seeing too far. Their bare limbs almost obscured the cloudless sky. Everywhere shade touched, frost covered. Alice breathed out in a puff to see her breath again and smiled at the small cloud.

"Don't tell me you all aren't this cold in New York." He nudged her shoulder with his as he walked by. "I've heard too much about Nor'easters to believe you."

She smiled at his teasing. "You have a point. We've had heavy snows in the past few years. Lovely, but difficult to get around all the same."

"We get weather like that, too." He tilted his head to the north. "Come on. I'll show you where I'll bet the boys tried to skate."

Alice did as he suggested, the wind whipping up as she regretted leaving behind her bonnet. Her ears already ached. While she followed, her eyes kept focusing in on his broad shoulders far more than on the surrounding forest. His torso tapered nicely to a slim waist and she enjoyed how his pants hinted at the leg muscles underneath. She would need to know more about him before understanding why Mrs. Dryden had left. Right now, she couldn't imagine running away from Jack for any reason.

She glanced away from him, her face hot despite the chill. His good looks and kind demeanor weren't related, and she needed to stay focused on finding the Hayses their best possible home. Daydreaming about Mr. Dryden helped no one. Alice shook her head as if to loosen the overly fresh thoughts about him. She needed to know his plans for a future without the children. "Do you want to stay here even if the adoption falls through? Or if Mrs. Dryden returns home?"

He paused until she closed in to walk beside him. "I, well, my mind has changed in the past week and more so in the past day." Giving her a side glance, he added, "Now, instead of accepting whatever decision you make, I intend on doing everything I can to keep the children with me. Ellie's return is a moot point now. My focus is on signing the adoption papers."

"Oh?" Alice snorted a little, thinking he showed some sass in assuming he could influence her decisions so easily. "I'm tempted to refuse your request if only to see what you'd do."

"Just as I thought." Jack knelt by a wide creek, complete with a gaping hole in the ice. "Trust them to find one of the most dangerous places to be this morning."

Making a mental note to return to the idea of refusing the adoption, Alice took the bait and asked, "Dangerous? The water seems to be shallow enough. They couldn't drown."

He straightened, slowly and favoring one knee. "No, but it deepens and thins on the other side. I'd bet neither would get a good dunking, but enough to give them the flu or chills."

Alice turned toward the house, unable to see it through the trees. "I reckon the walk back would do them no good if they were iced over." She refocused on him as he put more of his weight gingerly on one leg. "Are you all right?"

"Fine and getting better every day." He looked up at her with a grin. "Lady, Ellie's horse, nudged me forward on the way to the feed trough last month, and I took a hard tumble. I forget about my knee until the morning turns especially cold."

She leaned forward to get a better look at his knee. One of the sisters gave lessons in first aid, and Alice wanted to help. She put an arm around him, ready to support his weight if necessary. "Are you in pain? Do you need to lean against me on the way back?"

"I'm good. It just doesn't want to move when I want to go." He grinned, looking from her shoulder against his to her eyes. "It's doing better every day, I promise. Let me show you the barn."

Embarrassed, Alice let go of him. "Mm-hm." She kept up with him on their trek back to the house. The trail narrowed as before, and she let him lead a couple of times. As they neared the house, she asked, "You have a well and a creek. Does either ever run dry?"

"Not since we've—I've—been here," he replied as they veered off toward the barn. "The creek threatens to in late August, but there's always enough to wash laundry."

She nodded, impressed by the red barn, large now that she was closer. "I've read about barn raising in books. Did your neighbors help?"

"They did, and I return the favor as often as I can." He pulled open the large door. "Which is every time they ask. I'm lucky I have my health."

Her daydreams of Jack helping build something in the summer and probably without a shirt left her a little breathless. She frowned at the reaction and tried to refocus on staying impartial. He was still a married man and every base thought about him was a sin. Only, Alice began to argue in her mind as she walked into the wooden building, his wife was gone, and he didn't seem to think she'd return.

"It's not the biggest barn in the county but does the job for now." He closed the door behind them and continued in to meet up with her. "I do have plans for a few additions to this building and the house."

"It's rather dark in here," she said. Barely any sunlight streamed in from between the boards.

"I have plans to cut a window next spring." He went over to where a pane of glass rested against the wall. "Everything and everyone is ready for better weather."

The air was somewhat warmer than outside, enough for her to smell the straw, oats, and horse. She continued to where Shep was in his stall, an empty space beside him where Ellie's horse should have been. "I've read reports by agents on the types of homes we send children to and have even seen a few for myself." She turned to him in the dim rays shining in from the half-open door. "None of them have been as lovely as yours. Bigger, smaller, more and less developed, but your farm is one fit for a gallery painting."

"I'm pleased you think so, Miss McCarthy." He walked to the horse and began scratching the animal's nose. "I didn't know agents went into detail on anything."

Something seemed off in his statement. Not from him, but from the process the local agents used. "Yours should have let you read his report before sending it to us. Let you check for inaccuracies or to rebut opinions."

"He, um," Jack said before clearing his throat. "Well, you'll meet Mr. Donovan for yourself when we go into town later today."

"Good. We can compare notes on what you can provide and if you're able to parent the Hays children alone." She paused. "If your wife returns, I don't suppose you'll have any problems being a father after all."

"I don't expect so." Jack pulled off his gloves, shoving them into a pocket. "How about we go back to the house? The others are probably wondering where we are and why we're letting breakfast get cold."

Alice laughed at the idea of them sitting around, merely watching the food until she and Jack returned. "Or worse, eating everything yet again, so nothing is wasted."

He paused before closing the barn door. "Dang, hadn't thought of that. We'd better go in and salvage what we can."

She followed, a little surprised when first one, then another icy pellet hit her head. Just as she opened her mouth to ask if he'd felt it, too, a tinkling sound of sleet rained down on them.

"Uh-oh," he said, reaching for her hand. "We'd better hurry."

Alice instinctively held on to him, his cool touch offset by his strength. She kept up as he jogged with her to the back door of his home. "Goodness," she said once inside. "Thank you for your help."

"You're welcome, and Charlotte, did you manage to save us any of this second batch of breakfast?"

"Yes, Mr. Dryden." She returned his grin and stepped back from the stove as he approached. "I've been keeping the eggs warm and the boys away."

She peered into the bedrooms' open doorways. "They're outside in this mess?"

The back door burst open before anyone could reply and both boys rushed in. Conner began, "We were getting pebbles to play with."

"And then it started raining down on us," his brother finished.

"Pebbles," Jack asked.

"For marbles. We had to leave ours behind."

When Jack frowned at her, Alice squirmed at his disapproval. "They weren't the boys' marbles, but everyone's. Community property teaches them sharing."

His face not softening, he nodded. "I see. Good thing I'm prepared." He turned to the children. "The bottom drawer in the girls' bedroom is for you all. Actually, the whole dresser is for your use, Charlotte's, too."

All three looked to Alice first before she smiled. "Go and see what he has for you." They hurried off, and she went to where Jack stood by the stove. "Since we're here until the storm lets up, why don't we eat and talk about how your home visits with the agent went? I have a feeling I need to know more."

"Um, sure." He handed her a plate from the shelf. "Only, I don't suppose you're going to like everything you hear."

Alice dished up her breakfast. "I imagine I won't, judging by what you've said so far." She sat in the chair he pulled out for her and waited to eat until he settled in, too. He didn't look at her as he dug into his food. Their coffee now cold, she stood, the chair scraping on the wooden floor. Jack glanced up, ready to stand as well. "No, I'll refresh our drinks." She did so, adding, "I seem to remember Mr. Donovan saying you and your wife had a perfect home for children and a healthy, wholesome atmosphere." Alice sat, waiting until he'd swallowed before asking him, "Did he happen to know this firsthand, or at only your say-so?"

"A little bit of both." Jack put his elbows on the table and interlaced his fingers. "Harry and I go way back. He's been out here for dinner a couple of times."

"Hm." Dinner with him and his missus. Alice took a drink of coffee, but the bitter taste was in her mind, not on her tongue. She asked, "But nothing within the past year or so?"

"We've been busy."

"I see." She cut into the second egg. The food was perfect. Alice glanced at him while she chewed. He also ate, his expression distant. She supposed a marriage unraveling kept a couple too busy to have guests. "Had he ever met Mrs. Dryden?"

"Sure. Several times." He wiped his mouth with a napkin. "She went to town with me nearly every trip."

She didn't want to ask, especially since the answer might keep him from being allowed to adopt, but needed to know for sure. "He's aware Mrs. Dryden has returned home?"

Jack glanced at the bedroom door before responding. "No. No one except us knows what happened." He stared down at his plate. "It's not something a man brags about."

Her heart ached for him, and she couldn't imagine the lonely days he'd spent between her leaving and their arriving. Alice resisted taking his hand in hers, settling for replying, "I expect not."

Pausing for a moment, he said, "I should have known she'd leave long before she did. Now that I know what happened, the signs were all there."

"Oh?"

"Keeping most of her clothes in her trunk. Packing things away for just in case. Journaling. Lots and lots of journaling." He shook his head. "After all the times we argued, she'd threaten to go back home." Jack stared at his callused hands. "People say things they don't mean when they're angry. At least, I do. I thought she was the same way."

She clasped her hands in her lap. If Jack were any one of the children she'd helped care for back home, Alice would hug him and say everything would work out fine. The idea of holding him in such a way left her embarrassed. Clearing her throat to dispel the sudden longing for him, she smiled. "Things happen for a reason. Have you sent Mrs. Dryden a letter or telegraph, asking her to come home?"

"Telegraph, yes." He stood, taking their plates and cutlery. "Ellie has been very clear. She's not coming back."

Alice stared at him. He didn't look at her. Dumbfounded over how he'd not told her upfront about asking his wife to return home, she numbly asked, "Are you sure she said those exact words?"

CHAPTER 8

Jack didn't answer her for a moment, staring out at the weather with a squint. Alice wiped her mouth with a napkin. "I suppose I'm too forward, and I'm sorry." She picked up their empty dishes, adding them to the pail. "Your thoughts are none of my business."

"All I know is what she replied." He turned to face her and stopped, his gaze settling beyond where she stood. "She's done with everything out here, doesn't want any of us..."

When he trailed off, she followed where he stared and saw the children in the doorway. Each child's expression full of disappointment broke her heart. Charlotte stared down at the rag doll in her hands while Conner unwound a yo-yo's string. Carter crossed his arms and scowled. She couldn't bear it if they started crying. Alice smiled. "That's too bad because you are all the best family. We'll merely determine a solution that's best for everyone without her."

Alice regretted not turning on her heel and getting back on the train the instant she didn't see Mr. Dryden waiting for them. She should have known they were all rolling toward an emotional tar pit in going home with him. Now, everyone was counting on the adoption, including her. "Now, then, no more negativity. If the storm lets up this afternoon, we might go into town and talk with Mr....?" She looked to Jack for the agent's name.

"Donovan."

She nodded, now remembering. "Donovan, and get everything sorted out."

"Won't you let us stay?" Charlotte asked while coming over and leaning on Alice. "Mr. Dryden is alone, and we don't need a mother."

Carter stepped forward. "She's right. You know we'll do fine without one. We can all stay and help Pa on our farm."

Jack strode over and scooped up the boy as if he were a five-pound sack of flour. "First of all, if I'm going to be your pa, you have to know there's no sassing a lady like Miss Alice allowed. Drydens have manners." He smiled at the other two children. "And since she does need convincing, all of us must be on our best behavior, so she'll let you three stay on as my family."

He let Conner slide to the floor and took the dish bucket from Alice. "Grab your coats, and we'll do some chores, so she'll see how well we work together. We won't give her a chance to say no."

Faster than she'd ever been able to motivate them, the children ran back into the bedroom. The toys thudded on the wood floor, and the three rushed to the coat rack. Carter finished first, grabbed the bucket from Jack, and yelled, "I win!" as he ran out of the door.

"Be careful!" Alice hollered after them as they disappeared. She went to the door for herself and peered out. Carter must have handed off the dishes because Charlotte carried them while both boys ran and skidded along the frozen ground. The sleet had left a hard, grainy film on grass and dirt alike. She shivered and closed the door. They'd all be frozen by the time they returned.

She fastened the latch and went to the stove. Alice only found embers when peeking inside, so she piled fresh wood on the fire. In the daylight, she noticed a layer of dust not visible in the twilight or even early morning sun. She grabbed one of the boy's unused napkins and began dusting shelves and windowsills. The windows themselves could use a cleaning, but she didn't know for sure where Jack kept the vinegar or if he even had any. "Surely he does," she muttered while dusting breakfast crumbs from the table into her hand.

Alice went into Charlotte's and her bedroom. The toys strewn everywhere didn't surprise her. She smiled and put the marbles left on the bed back into their cloth pouch. Charlotte's doll went back into the drawer with the yo-yo and carved wooden horse. She traced her fingertips along the animal's back, wondering if Jack had made or bought the toy. Placing it in the bottom dresser, she closed the drawer before dusting the top.

The bed rails were as smooth as the dresser's surface and didn't snag the napkin. She wiped the front windowsill first. At the back window, she watched as the children went into the distant chicken coop and heard Jack's heavier feet when he stomped onto the back porch. She wiped down the sill in a hurry before entering the main room as he did. His face ruddy from the cold, Alice smiled at him and said, "That didn't take long."

"Not with the four of us working." He held out the pail full of water and dishes. "Trade me this for the water bucket? I'll stay here to keep from tracking in the ice."

"Certainly." Alice reached out for the handle, her bare hand brushing his chilled fingertips. "Oh," she murmured before setting down the dishes, "you're freezing." She took his hand in both of hers. "Did you forget your gloves?"

"I didn't want to get them wet."

"You don't wash dishes outside, do you?" she asked while rubbing some feeling back into his frozen skin. "I've added fuel to the stove, so we can heat the water and wash them properly." She let go of him and beckoned for his other hand. "Maybe you should wear your gloves on this next trip and tell the children to put on theirs as well." She rubbed his skin as she would her own after a time in the bitter chill. "Goodness, did you wash your hands outside, too?"

"Not intentionally." He grinned. "I'll be sure to tell the boys when they're older about how to get a pretty girl to hold their hand."

Alice gasped and let go of him, her face hot in the already-warm room. "Oh! Well, you were cold and I, um...never mind." She clasped her fingers in front of her, uncertain how to gracefully apologize. "I should have treated you like the adult you are, and I'm sorry."

"No need to be." Jack put on his gloves and went for the water bucket. "I didn't know how numb I was until you warmed me up just now."

She nodded, the heat in her cheeks still burning. "I'm glad." Alice picked up the dish bucket. "I'll take care of these." She turned to the stove and set the pail on top to heat. His steps sounded across the common room and away from her.

When the door shut, she peeked behind her, and her shoulders slumped. What had she been thinking, caressing the man's hands as she had? Alice shook her head. She hadn't been thinking at all, just concerned at how pale his fingertips were. Anyone would have done the same. She scooped up the dust cloth and went to the last room, Jack's bedroom, to clean.

Alice paused at the doorway. The bed was made but barely, and even from where she stood, a light layer of dust covered the flat surfaces. She bit her lip. Accidental hand-holding was one thing but invading someone's privacy was another. A bedroom in a public place like a hotel or the orphanage was easy. She knew the rules for those situations. Walking into the sleeping area of a man in his own home seemed far too intimate for an adoption agent. The back door opening again startled her, and she dropped the cloth with a little yelp.

Carter ran in with Conner, followed by their sister. "Jack let us feed Shep and bust the ice for the cattle."

Alice picked up the napkin and grimaced at the shoe prints on the floor. Wiping their feet on rainy days would be a habit they'd need to learn by spring. "I suppose your adventures outside are why there's a mess inside?"

"Maybe," Conner replied as all three eased back toward the door and kicked off their shoes.

She laughed at the guilty expressions. "I was saving the mopping for last, and you all can help." Ignoring the boys' groans, Alice continued, "Conner can sweep one bedroom, Charlotte the main area, and Carter the last bedroom as soon as I'm finished dusting."

Jack walked in on her last few words. His eyebrows rose at seeing the wet floor and pile of shoes. Giving Alice a sheepish grin, he kicked off his boots. "You all know you're my guests and not my hired help, don't you?"

"We do. However, if you're kind enough to give us a place to stay while you and I work out the adoption, we're kind enough to help."

He walked into the kitchen part of the main room. "I can tell the difference already." After he set the bucket of water by the stove, he went to the window. "Yes, much better." Jack grinned at her. "What's next?"

"Washing dishes and dusting your bedroom, maybe?" She twisted the cloth in her hands. "I wanted to ask before barging in."

"You're always welcome in my—" He paused before chuckling. "I mean to say, you're always welcome to clean anything in here. Bedrooms included."

"If you're sure I won't be invading your privacy..."

"You won't be." He walked into his bedroom. "Come on. No need to be shy. We have chaperones."

Her cheeks seemed to stay flushed around this man, Alice thought as she followed him into the bedroom. The walls were as freshly built as in Charlotte's and her room. She looked through the windows. They needed cleaning, of course, but gave a good view of the front and back of the house from the bed. "You built both rooms at the same time, didn't you?"

"I did. I knew Ellie and I would want"—he paused, chuckling before saying—"our privacy after the children arrived."

"Uh-huh," she said, giving him a wry grin. Not knowing what else to say, Alice dusted the northern window first while Jack straightened the bedcovers a little better. "I suppose, now, privacy is a moot point."

"Exactly." He retrieved a sock from the dresser and began wiping dust from the south window. "Thank you for helping me in here. I never thought about cleaning the windows."

She turned to the center of the room and watched as Jack wiped side to side. "The outside will need vinegar. It helps with water spots."

"That might be something saved for spring cleaning. I'm ready to warm up for a bit."

"I can imagine." She began dusting his dresser, smiling when spotting the letter she'd sent him sitting on top of a small stack of correspondence. Her cursive could use some practice.

He went over to her. "You can dust under them, or I can. They're just letters I need to take care of." He picked them up and held hers apart from the rest. "Especially this one. It's my highest priority."

Looking at the others, she tilted her head. "I don't know. One of them seems to be typewritten, and I think the last is a telegram."

The merriment faded from his expression. "They're something I can't fix or change." He held up one, placing her letter on the dresser. "This is a divorce decree, and it needs my signature to make it final." He laid it on top of her letter.

"Divorce? You have the actual document? I don't know if I've ever met someone who'd do such a thing."

He frowned at the letter with its heavy type and wrinkles. "I never thought she'd leave for good. I should have known after the first couple of years. She tried to be happy, but after I'd finished building new rooms onto the house, she saw we weren't going back east."

Alice stared at him for a moment, not sure how to comfort him. If she said the new wood smell and hard work would appeal to nearly any other woman, would he think she was patronizing him? Or would he only care what Ellie thought? She didn't know for sure and offered, "So, she's made up her mind, and you truly can't charm her back home? There's been so much work done on the homestead. Maybe if you explained to her how you're building a life for you and your children, she'd reconsider."

Jack shook his head, a slight smile hanging around his lips as he took a folded piece of paper from his pocket. He straightened it out before placing it and the Western Union receipt on top of the legal document. "And this is the reply I received when asking Ellie to forget the divorce."

Alice read the single word "No" typed on the wrinkled paper. "Oh, goodness, Jack," she whispered. Ellie had responded over a week ago, judging by the stamped date. "I'm sorry."

"So am I, except, if she was unhappy enough to walk out without looking back, maybe we're both better off she's gone." Their gazes met in the dresser's mirror. "I still want to adopt the Hays children and give them a good life away from the city. Only, they'll have to make do with a father until I find a woman desperate enough to marry me."

She broke their connection first, walking over to the other side of the bed to put distance between them. The words lingered in her mind, and she had to argue, "I don't think a woman would have to be desperate."

He put his hands in his pockets and shrugged. "I suppose you're right. Maybe some small-town gal would want to live out here with me, us. Some little ol' woman who'd consider this home a palace."

Between what he was saying and the twinkle in his eye, Alice frowned. "So, you have a new wife already picked out?" She walked up to him, arms crossed and tapping her foot. "No moss growing on your heart, is there? Have you signed the divorce yet?"

"Not yet on both counts." His grin grew wider. "Give me some time before marrying me off to the first woman you find."

"*I* find?" She shook her head. "I've found you your children." Alice couldn't find anything else to dust and went to the front-facing window. Looking out, she added, "I'm not a matchmaker."

He walked up behind her and nudged her with his shoulder. "Too bad, because I already love them and would probably love any woman you picked for me."

Jack was standing far too close to her, and his teasing was too charming. She stepped to the side, putting her hands on her hips. She floundered for what to argue back. "I, well, I don't think it's appropriate for me to pick your wife. Some things are beyond my abilities."

Jack laughed. "Somehow, I doubt that." He held up a hand before she could add another rebuttal. "Fine, I'll choose my own wife, and I'll get started after I see what everyone's doing. Quiet children and loud chickens always mean trouble."

She watched as he left the room. Alice waited but didn't hear any voices. Curious, she stepped out into the main area to find Jack exiting her bedroom. "Are they all right?"

"They're asleep."

"What? Those lazybones." She tossed the dust rag onto the table. "They can't sleep all day."

Just as she walked past Jack, he grabbed her arm and pulled her to him. Her forward momentum carried her up against his chest, and she let out a squeak. He grinned and steadied her, holding on to her shoulders. "Wait a minute, little lady. You're doing no such thing."

"I am, too," she mumbled. His closeness unnerved her. She stared at his lips, aware how if she lifted her chin a couple of inches, they'd be able to kiss.

"No, you're letting them sleep." His grip on her relaxed and his hands fell to his sides. "In fact, the sky is darkening again, and my bet is we'll get round two of sleet this afternoon. You might as well follow the children's example and get some rest yourself."

"I'm not tired right now." As soon as the words left her, Alice yawned. "I'm not. You talking about sleep is making me sleepy, that's all."

He put his arm around her, turning Alice toward his bedroom. "Come on. Lie down for a little while and rest your eyes."

"Where will you be?"

"In the main room, doing dishes and working on a project or two."

"I suppose a nap couldn't hurt." She yawned again. "I am rather tired from the trip." Alice took a few steps back before asking, "You'll wake me when I need to do something around here? Fix lunch, or dinner if you don't have a midday meal?"

"Sure. I'll do that."

She gave him one last smile before going to his bedroom. Alice stared at the bed for a moment, wondering which side to sleep on. When cleaning earlier, she'd not taken the time to notice where he'd slept and where the boys had been. The sleet began falling again, and she decided to stop dithering. Jack wouldn't care and had said as much already.

Alice slid in under the covers, the cotton sheets cold. The heavy quilt left her feeling cocooned, and she snuggled in. The pillow smelled like him: sun, leather, and lavender. Alice sighed, knowing she'd picked the wrong and very appealing side, but not caring. Alone, no distractions, and resting where he slept every night would keep her awake and longing for him.

CHAPTER 9

Jack glanced up from the leather strap. Someone was snoring, but he wasn't sure which person it was. He stood slowly, so the chair's legs didn't scrape loudly against the wooden floor. Avoiding the squeaky board, he went to the children's room first and checked in on them. He'd expected all three to be lying neatly head to headboard, but no. They'd been playing with a doll and wooden farm animals, nodding off where they were on the bed.

He grinned when figuring Alice must be the one making all the racket. Checking in on her found the young woman on his side of the bed, face up, with her forearm over her eyes. Truth be told, he'd heard louder gargles from his brother and pa, but not from such a lovely and refined woman like her.

Shaking his head and trying not to chuckle, Jack went back to the table and the strip of leather. He sat, resuming his work on the new bridle. He'd planned on this one being for Ellie's horse. He paused, his hands faltering for a moment. Alice and the children had kept his mind occupied almost too well today. He brushed off the pause and continued working the leather.

Telling Alice about the divorce papers and Ellie's response hadn't hurt as much as he'd expected. He'd had fun egging her on a little but not too much to find a wife for him. He tested the inside smoothness between a ring and the leather loop to make sure nothing would irritate Shep's face.

When he finished his project, Jack planned to break out his financial ledger. He'd like to make sure each child had their own horse, and Charlotte would need a sidesaddle. Imagining her being his real daughter brought a smile to his face. He stared out the window at the clearing sky. A lot had happened in less than a day. And tomorrow? His smile faded. Everything depended on what Donovan said, and Alice accepted, for the adoption.

Refocusing on his work, he finished up what he could on the bridle and set it aside on his work shelf. His stomach growled while he retrieved his ledger and ink set. If he was hungry, the others would be, too.

He grabbed his coat and threw it on while on his way to the root cellar. Jack pulled open the door, leaving it open to let in the light. Seed and eating potatoes were in small barrels to the back, and all his preserves sat on shelves built into the front walls. The warm earth smelled good, leaving him more than ready for spring plowing.

His hand paused on its way to grabbing a jar of beans and carrots. Did Charlotte know how to can vegetables already? He'd taught Ellie during their first year here. Jack didn't mind helping another person with farm work. He put a few potatoes in his pocket, ready for tomorrow evening to be here already. By then, he'd know if he had a family or a lonely homestead.

Jack straightened his back. If Alice and Donovan needed convincing about his parenting skills, he was up to the challenge. He'd taken care of his father and brother after his mother died. He'd come out here and built a respectable homestead, and he'd been a decent husband to Ellie.

He stopped halfway to the house and stared at the jar of vegetables in his hand. All right, so his former wife might not agree with his assessment, but still. He loved, or rather had loved her, had been faithful, rarely drank liquor, and helped her become a good farmer's wife. And now? Jack sighed and stared up at the gloomy sky. Now, he still had his home and what he wanted for a family. He just needed to keep both for good.

The front door opened with a creak and he eased inside. Before too long, Jack had the vegetables simmering in the cookpot. He heard the squeaky board and turned to see Conner approach. Giving the soup a stir, he said to the boy, "Good morning, sleepyhead. How was your nap?"

Conner rubbed his eyes as he went to the stove. "Good. I was only going to close my eyes for a minute."

"That tends to happen sometimes."

He peeked into the pot. "Smells good."

"Vegetable stew."

The boy didn't budge. "Mm-hm. Looks like a lot of 'em." He looked up at Jack. "Are you sure we need that many?"

"You don't have to eat them all yourself. I'm sure the others will want some, too."

Carter walked in, a copy of his brother, and went to Jack's other side, asking, "Hey, are we going to town today?" He stood on tiptoes to peer at the food. "After supper?"

"After supper what?" Charlotte asked from the doorway. "Mmm, smells good. Where's Miss McCarthy?"

"She's resting," Jack replied. "We'll probably go to town tomorrow after breakfast."

"Will we wear our clothes or yours?" Conner asked.

He laughed. "Probably your own. How about we go check on the animals for the evening and bring your pants in to thaw?" Jack stood and smiled at Charlotte. "Want to help?"

The girl nodded while going to where her shoes were by the back door. "Do you want me to wake Miss McCarthy?"

"Not yet. After we're done, if she's not up we can wake her." He waited until everyone wore their coats before leading them outside. The gray sky banked in and stilled the air as he picked their way to the henhouse.

Carter came up beside him. "How do you keep the chickens warm?"

"We never noticed a stove," Charlotte added.

Jack opened the door and ushered them all in. "As much hay as I keep in here, I like the hens not having a fire going." He went over to the water pan. Despite tacking up the wired openings with oilcloth, a solid film of ice had formed on top of the chicken's water since the morning. "Most of the time, I just have to break the thin ice during evening chores." He used a small hammer to punch a hole for the birds to drink from before placing the tool back on a couple of nails to keep it off the floor.

Wanting to teach them skills and help them feel like a part of the farm's success, Jack said, "Carter, why don't you give them a scoop of corn and Conner can bring in a couple handfuls of hay for the floor." He smiled while Charlotte reached out to pet a hen. "And you, young lady, can gather eggs for us."

She nodded, reaching in under the chicken. "We can have biscuits and gravy for breakfast tomorrow."

Jack's stomach growled as he nodded. "I'll be sure to bring in some ham from the smoke shed." He stepped out, the air noticeably cooler in the dimming light. "Let's check on the bigger animals before dinner." A soft lantern glow shone through his home's windows. Alice was awake and hopefully stirring the soup he'd started.

Charlotte hugged the eggs close to her. "I'll take these inside."

"Good, and check on dinner?"

"Yes." She gave him a shy smile and headed toward the house. "Miss Alice and I will set the table, too."

Before Jack could reply to her, Conner asked him, "Will you teach us how to ride Shep someday?"

Carter pulled the barn door back, adding, "When we're old enough we can saddle him for ya."

He let the boys lead the way to his horse. How everything concerning their adoption hovered in doubt kept him silent for a moment, thinking. No one could plan or count on anything until they'd talked to Donovan and convinced Alice they needed to stay. "I expect you can." He nodded at Shep's stall, grinning when both boys reached in to pet the animal. "What do you think we do first?"

"Check his water," Carter said.

Conner added, "And give him oats and apples."

"Good answers." He unlatched the door. "How about Carter checks the water and Conner can get a can of oats for him." Jack patted Shep's neck as the horse nudged him. "I'll show you where the apples are in the cellar, and you can give him slices tomorrow morning." The animal left him once the oats began hitting the trough. Jack eased out of the stall. "When you're done here, come over and help me check the cows."

They answered him with mumbles, too focused on Shep to be polite. Jack shook his head, amused and happy they liked his horse. He went to his cows, using a shovel to tap through the thin skin of ice as the boys came over to see what he was doing. Stepping back so his cows could get a drink, he said,

"Hello, ladies. You're looking lovely today." One of the boys snickered next to him, and he grinned at Carter. "These here are my best mothers so far. We'll have three new calves in the spring."

"So, you'll have six cows? That's all?" the boy asked.

Conner came up to Jack's other side. "We saw farms with too many cows to count."

"Back east, I'll bet, and fewer as you were closer to Liberty?" he asked, and they nodded. "The country is still recovering from locusts in '74 and '75." He scooped up a large can of feed mix and dumped it in their food trough. "We'd been here almost a year when it hit and were almost wiped out. Mrs. Dryden wanted to go back home then and there, but I convinced her to stay, and the homestead did get better."

Not letting either of them ask about his soon-to-be former wife, he hurried to add, "We planted a garden late, and everything grew like weeds, including the weeds. I replanted what I could, sold down the stock, and harvested locust eggs for a dollar a barrel."

"No," Carter said. "You harvested locust eggs?"

"They build nests like birds?" Conner asked. "Must have been some big grasshoppers out here."

He laughed and gave one of the cows a final scratch on the head before heading for the door. "Come on, I'll tell you more about the swarms over supper because I'll bet it's ready by now."

CHAPTER 10

ALICE SMILED AT CHARLOTTE. PRIDE MIGHT NOT BE encouraged at the Home, but she couldn't help but be proud of the girl. "It seems Mr. Dryden is as good a cook as you are."

The girl breathed in deep over the cookpot. "I'd say better." She went to the bedroom she shared with Alice, saying over her shoulder, "When do you think they'll be done, and do we need to wait for them before eating?"

She chuckled, not blaming her impatience a bit. "Yes, we do need to share with the boys. Remember we have manners, even out here." Charlotte mumbled something in reply and Alice wasn't sure exactly what. Judging by the tone, maybe it was best she didn't know. She drummed her fingertips on the table a few times before deciding to at least set out the bowls and spoons. Done with the small tasks, she looked at the stew again, choosing to add the last little bit of their water to the broth.

They'd want fresh water, too, if not hot tea as well. She took the bucket to the back door where her coat hung. Alice slipped into her shoes and coat as the door opened and the boys rushed in, panting. Her exclaiming, "Feet, gentlemen," stopped them in their tracks and they went back to the door with frowns. She struggled to not laugh at how adorable both boys were and said, "Good job. You don't want to mop before dinner, do you?"

"No, ma'am," they mumbled while kicking off his shoes.

She began to say something when the door opened again. Jack stood there with a bigger bucket than hers. Cold reddened his cheeks, and his eyes twinkled. Every time she saw him, he seemed to be a little more handsome than the moment before. She nodded at his pail. "Seems we have the same idea."

"Great minds and all that." He reached for her bucket. "Let me take yours to fill."

"I can help," she offered while putting the container behind her skirts. When he grinned at her, Alice's face grew warm. "You can probably handle everything yourself, but I've done very little today."

He held open the door wider for her. "Come along, then, and tell me what gave you such a wrong idea."

Alice laughed at him being so blunt. "Excuse me? Wrong? That's not possible."

Jack nudged her shoulder with his as they stepped off the porch. "Sorry, ma'am, I meant to say 'slightly mistaken' instead."

Her foot slipped on a slick patch, and she grabbed his arm. "Goodness!" Her heart pounded at the near fall.

After wrapping his arm around her, Jack pulled her to his side. "This is always a problem when the weather is freezing. You don't notice the slope until you're flat on your behind, counting the clouds or stars."

She glanced up through the bare branches until refocusing on the ground ahead. "Thank you for the rescue. You can let go now."

"I will when we get to the creek. In the meantime, let me list how much you've helped around the farm today."

"This won't take long," she quipped and grinned when he chuckled.

"You brought the children to me, and I know Charlotte will have us all fatter than a spoiled pig. Then, you cleaned up all traces of my neglect while I wallowed in pity."

Alice tried to focus more on his words and less on how a man was hugging her. "You lost your wife. You're allowed to mourn her if she's truly gone."

He stopped their walk and turned her to face him. "I did mourn her. I wanted her back. I needed what we had together."

His change in verb tense urged on her slim thread of hope. "You did. Not do?"

He shook his head slightly. "Not anymore. There are plenty of single gals at church, in town, heck, even where I grew up. I could send a letter or go and talk to any of them to come here and be a mother to the children." He stared at her for a second or two. "And I'd want her to be a wife to me." He swallowed, not breaking their gaze. "I don't want just anyone, though. I want someone I can love and who'll love me enough to stay forever."

Emotions jumped around her like shotgun pellets in a shaken preserves jar. He couldn't mean her as his love, yet his intent stare led her to believe he did. She had a life waiting for her back east, and Jack knew that. Alice had to counter his assertions with, "Forever is a very long time.

What if the woman you love can't live here? What if she has responsibilities to others, first?" The light in his eyes dimmed. She missed his warmth both literally and emotionally and leaned in closer to him. "The woman you care for may have no idea she's the one you're thinking of."

He moved a couple of inches nearer to her before saying, "If she doesn't, then I need to be a better communicator, don't I?"

She swayed a little toward him. "Oh, yes, telling her outright would be helpful."

"We'll be out here until tomorrow at this rate." Jack straightened. "Let's hurry up and get back before we're frozen in place."

He resumed guiding her to the water pump, and Alice watched as he filled his pail before setting it aside. She handed hers to him when he was ready. "About communication, I mean, most women would want to hear nice things about how pretty she is, how you can't live without her, and that she'd had your heart from the moment you two met." She took her full bucket from him. "I wouldn't be like a woman who'd want to hear such things, though."

Jack chuckled. "No? So, you'd be the one in a million who didn't want sweet talk and courting?"

She frowned, unhappy now since she'd talked him out of any sort of romance. Still, she'd made her bed and now had to lie in it. Alice lifted her chin, trying to look down her nose at him, somewhat difficult to do due to his height. "I'm much more practical. I'd rather hear about a man's plans and the ways I can help him realize our dreams. Love is nice, but it doesn't produce anything." He chuckled, and she asked, "Doesn't it?"

Giving her the smaller pail of water, he said, "For couples without children, you might be right. Love isn't productive, but others? It's why the Hayses are in my home wondering when we're going to return so they can eat."

His meaning hit Alice like a rock to her head, and her face burned with embarrassment over what she'd implied. "I didn't mean to be fresh by mentioning love and everything."

"I know you didn't," he said, putting his arm around her for the icy part of the path. "You turned so red I couldn't help but tease you."

"Yes, well, you're very good at getting me flustered," she retorted. Jack took his arm from around her, his hand sliding across her back. His solid strength gone as he stepped onto the porch, Alice followed him, already missing his touch.

He paused before opening the back door. "I didn't mean to offend you earlier," he said in a quiet voice. "I forgot how to act around a proper lady, I guess."

"You know my history," Alice replied as softly as he'd spoken. "I may be proper, but I'm hardly a lady."

"I disagree." He set down the bucket and held her by the shoulders. "You're a fine woman."

Alice stared into his eyes, lost and unable to look away. She wanted the longing in his face to be real and for her. His lips parted, and she leaned forward. "You're a good man, too." Before either of them could protest, she kissed him.

The moment they touched, she shivered. He deepened the kiss, and she almost panicked at how perfectly they fit together. She moaned and stepped up against him, melting into his strength.

He groaned, giving her a bone-crushing squeeze. "No," he whispered against her lips. "This isn't right."

Not wanting to let him go, she wound her fingers into the hair at the back of his neck and pulled him closer. "It's perfect," she replied before resuming their kiss.

He deepened their contact as if hungry for more. One of his hands slid down her back, stopping when he touched her hip. He paused, withdrawing and stepping back. "I'm sorry. Let's go inside." Jack turned on a heel and left her there.

The door shutting snapped her awake from the trance. She bit her bottom lip, wondering if the last few seconds had been a dream or a nightmare. Alice put a hand to her mouth. Considering how she was alone in the bitter cold yet her lips were still warm, maybe kissing him had been both.

She needed to apologize for being so bold, yet she wasn't sorry. Alice picked up her pail and went inside. The warmth enveloped her as snugly Jack's hug had. The three children were seated at the table, eating dinner, and all stared at her with guilty expressions. She smiled. "Thank you for starting without me." Alice kicked off her shoes. "I wouldn't want to make you wait on my account."

Jack put down two bowls. "I've served your dinner already."

After a slight search, she noticed his larger bucket next to the stove and held up her pail. "Do I need to take this out to the livestock for you?"

He walked over and took the bucket from her, saying, "No, this will be for us. I'll take the larger one out to them later tonight." Jack set it down next to his. "Come on and eat before it gets cold."

She nodded and put her coat on its hook. "What do you think?" she asked the children. "Is he good or should we let Charlotte take over for now?"

The boys looked from Jack to their sister. Charlotte swallowed and said, "I think I'll let him cook from now on."

Alice settled into her chair and took a bite. The potatoes, carrots, green beans, and peas in a tomato base tasted better than anything she'd eaten back east. "Mmm," she said. "You're wonderful, but I agree. Mr. Dryden is an excellent cook."

"Does this mean no biscuits and gravy tomorrow?" Jack asked Charlotte.

She grinned. "I like your plan better. I can always make eggs and bacon the next day."

Alice stared down at her half-empty bowl. Tomorrow may be their last day here, weather permitting. She stirred the soup. Kissing Jack had thrown her dreams off-kilter. Worst of all, she'd have to confess to Father O'Brien as soon as she arrived home. Ellie might be gone for good, but the divorce wasn't signed. Her stomach twisted. Would a confession even help, or was she damned forever?

Jack stood and headed for the stove, saying, "Boys, why don't you two find your toys in the drawer and play with them? You too, Charlotte, and I'll clean up when Miss McCarthy is finished."

She glanced up in time to see Conner fling a green bean at Carter. The vegetable landed in the boy's hair, and Alice frowned. They knew better than to waste food in such a destructive way. "Excuse me?" She sat up straighter. "I don't know where you learned such unacceptable behavior, but I expect all this to stop this instant."

"Sorry, Miss Alice," Carter and Conner said in unison.

Standing, she added, "In fact, I think toys are for tomorrow, not tonight. I'd suggest you two clean up and go to bed."

"But we—" Conner began.

Alice held up a hand to stop the arguing in its tracks. "No. Since you're not sleepy, you'll have plenty of time to think about how wrong it is to waste food."

"I don't like green beans," Carter mumbled as he walked past her.

"That may be, but someone else here does, and you didn't consider other people." She ignored the further grumbling and Charlotte's smirk. "In fact, the three of you can get ready for bed and try to remember the lessons on good behavior we tried to teach you."

The amused expression slid from the younger girl's face as she followed her brothers before slipping into her bedroom. Alice waited until Jack settled back into his chair before saying, "I'm terribly sorry. Are you sure you want them to stay with you?"

He stared past her at the bedroom she and Charlotte shared. "I am. If a stray vegetable or two is the worst they give me, I can handle it."

Alice chuckled. "You do make a good point." She stared at him for a moment, desperately wishing they'd met under better circumstances. Tomorrow they'd finalize the adoption, probably in his and the children's favor, and she'd go home having kissed a married man. She stirred what little remained of her food and stared down at her food, suddenly ill.

Jack cleared his throat. "About earlier, I'm sorry."

"I am, too." She couldn't meet his gaze. "I was very wrong, and I apologize."

He leaned back in his chair, the wood giving a little squeak. "I enjoyed your mistake and would want another chance anytime you feel like making it again."

She looked up at him, hope and horror mixing with the food in her stomach. "I...you, you're still married, Jack." Alice pushed her bowl forward, the smell making her queasy. "Our kiss was a sin."

"I see." He took another bite, staring at the table as if in a trance while he ate.

"I'm glad you do, and I almost regret what I did."

"Almost?"

Alice frowned at what sounded like hope in his voice. "Well, I don't regret the kiss as much as the timing. You're not a free man, after all."

"What do you consider a free man, exactly?"

"One who isn't married in any way, of course."

"I understand and respect your opinion." He stood, taking his bowl. "It was sinful for us to embrace like we did."

She folded her hands in her lap and stared down at them. "Yes, it was." This time when he walked away, she didn't watch him leave. From what she heard, he stopped at the stove first before going on to his bedroom. Most of her was glad he saw the truth in what they'd done, but a small part wanted him to protest. To say their kiss was meant to be and declare his undying devotion for her.

Alice stood with her bowl and turned to put it in the water pail. Absorbed in her own thoughts, she'd not heard Jack return to the room. "Oh, I thought you were going to retire for the night."

He waved an envelope in his hand. "I am in a little while," he replied and went to where the ink and pen were stored. "There's something I need to do before we go to town tomorrow and I don't see the need to wait any longer."

Watching as he brought the writing tools to the kitchen table, Alice frowned. He couldn't sign the adoption papers until she'd spoken to Donovan. "Are you sure, because I don't think your signature will be valid."

Jack paused in dipping the pen. "My signature and date will be, even if I can't file anything with the courthouse at this hour." He continued, tapping off the extra ink and signing his name with a flourish.

She edged close enough to see "Divorce" as the paper's title. Alice crossed her arms, chilled all of a sudden. "Jack! Are you certain? What if Ellie changes her mind?"

He finished signing the date and said, "I'd been thinking about that myself." Jack set the pen aside and stood, walking up to Alice. "I've begged her to return. She gave me her answer, and I considered selling the farm and following her." He uncrossed her arms and put them around himself while his hands slid to her waist. "Thing is, you kissed me and interrupted all that."

"The children?"

"They started my new way of thinking, and you finished it for them." He leaned in to where their lips nearly touched. "Since I'm single on paper as well as in my heart, I want to see if the second time is as perfect as the first."

"This is wrong," she whispered.

He pressed his lips to hers with the lightest of touches. "Are you sure?"

Alice groaned with the effort of restraining herself and gave in to the need for more. She took his mouth in a kiss she'd needed since their last encounter ended. His hold on her tightened, and she buried her fingers in his hair. He was so tall and all male. She broke their lip-lock long enough to ask, "And tomorrow?"

"I'll file the decree, and we'll talk to Donovan about the adoption." He resumed kissing her for a few seconds before adding, "I want you to stay here with them. With me."

Intoxicated by his touch, Alice nodded at first. Her mind began clearing as she remembered her work in New York. Living in Missouri would be a dream compared to the city. Would a country life truly be what she wanted? Instead of helping hundreds of babies find new homes, she'd be living here with Jack and the children. "I...don't know if I can."

She stepped back, withdrawing from his arms. "I have my work at the Home to consider."

"Yes," he said, putting his clenched hands down. "You do. I was wrong to assume you'd abandon your life based on a couple of kisses from me. I'm sorry."

She wiped her lips. "We do seem to be apologetic today, don't we?" Alice gave a nervous laugh to help ease the scowl on his face. "Never mind. Let's focus on the children and finding them a good home with you. Agreed?"

"Yes, of course." He folded the divorce paper before placing it back into the envelope. "We'll have an early day tomorrow. I'd suggest getting some sleep."

She watched as he turned down the lanterns and asked him, "Shall I do the dishes?"

"Tomorrow." He went to his coat, putting it on before grabbing the heated pail of water for the animals. "I'll clean them up before breakfast," Jack added and left Alice in the waning glow of the wood stove without a backward glance.

She sighed. His kisses were beyond anything she'd ever imagined, but she had a commitment to the Home. Alice went to Charlotte's and her bedroom, finding her sleep dress by touch. She changed clothes and slid into bed, her heart still pounding.

Alice wanted to settle down here, be the woman in Jack's life. She'd never considered marrying so soon, wanting to wait. Maybe when the teasing about her being an old maid turned a little more serious, she'd fall in love. So many orphans waited back home for her. Other people could help them, certainly. Alice wasn't so naïve as to think the program would cease when she quit. Plus, other married people placed children. Sure, all the people escorting orphans were men, but still. She didn't mind being the first married woman.

After a couple of minutes lying there and trying to sleep, she turned to stare up at the ceiling. Here she was, already married to Jack in her imagination. She snorted a laugh before remembering to be quiet. No one upended their entire life for a man they'd known all of two days. She'd go into town, Donovan would vouch for Jack, papers would be signed, and she'd go home. Simple as that.

CHAPTER 11

JACK STIRRED THE GRAVY. THERE HAD TO BE A WAY TO convince Alice to stay a little longer, to see if they were as right for each other as their kisses had been last night. He checked the biscuits, taking them off the heat and lifting the lid on the Dutch oven. The boys were still joking about how stiff their pants had been this morning fresh off the clothesline. Both sets of pants were thawing, draped over a shelf near the stove.

Charlotte was outside, and he supposed Alice still slept. He'd have to go in and wake her since the sausage and gravy smell wasn't working its charm. Jack moved the pan to a lower heat and went to the second bedroom.

The door wasn't latched, and Jack looked in on her. He stopped in his tracks, stunned. Her hair fanned out over the pillow where she lay. She turned her head to him, sitting up and pulling the sheet close to her chest. He smiled. "Good morning."

She smiled. "Good morning. I didn't mean to sleep in."

"Don't worry about it." His heart thudded hard in his chest. She couldn't know he wanted to climb in bed with her and snuggle under the covers. He cleared his throat before saying, "Breakfast is almost ready, and I didn't want you to eat it cold."

"Thank you. The children?"

"Outside. I'll holler for them." He paused at the doorway, feeling the need to clean up any misunderstandings between them. "Last night—"

Alice shook her head. "Was lovely, but we both have our lives to live. I have my work back home, as you have yours here."

He went and sat on her side of the bed. "We do, but I want more. I want all of us together."

She bit her lip as he took her hand. "I don't know, Jack," she said. "You're asking me to give up my work. Would you be so willing to leave your farm?"

Jack let her hand slide from his. He gritted his teeth at first, hating to admit the truth until he finally said, "No, I wouldn't. You're right, and I understand why you must leave."

Her eyes shimmered, and she stared down at her lap for a moment before saying, "I'm sorry, I really am." Alice sniffed. "If you'll call the children in to eat breakfast, I'll get dressed for the day."

He stood, too aware of how little she wore and how intimate the bedroom had become. "Of course." Jack left for the back door. Instead of hollering for them, he decided to find the Hayses for himself.

The henhouse door stood ajar. He grinned, guessing who was in there. After getting there, he opened the coop and said, "Hello?" while peeking inside. He wasn't surprised to see Charlotte petting one of the tamer hens. If he didn't know better, he'd swear the bird was smiling at her. "Breakfast is ready. Have you seen the boys?"

She continued smoothing the feathers of a chicken sitting on a nest of eggs. "They went to play in the creek even after I told them not to."

"In the creek?" he said loud enough to startle everyone, including himself. "They know we're going to town today.

Alice will have a fit if they get as dirty as they were yesterday."

"Won't you be mad, too?"

"No, not too much." He laughed at her surprised expression. "You forget that I used to be a boy and always in trouble. My bet is Donovan remembers being just as ornery and will forgive a little bit of dirt."

She didn't look at him but at her new feathered friend. "Do you think he'll let us stay even if we're not perfectly good children for you?"

The question took him back. Jack knew he was going to be the best father possible. Things might get tough, but he had no doubts they'd work through it together. Charlotte's hand paused as she waited for his answer and he replied, "Yes, I think he will, and if he doesn't I'll just have to change his mind."

She turned from the hen and asked, "And Miss Alice?"

Alice McCarthy was a can of worms he'd deal with later. At least, his stomach felt like a tin full of nightcrawlers every time he thought about her going home. "I want her to stay, too, but she's her own person and must do what she thinks is best."

Charlotte gave him a slight smile. "She'll want us to stay with you, too."

Her statement made him realize he'd misunderstood her question. His measured answer had been to his own longing to keep Alice with him on the farm and didn't address the girl's fears about her own future. "Yes, sorry; of course, she does. She seems willing to let the adoption go through." He backed out of the coop. "I'd better check on the boys and make sure they haven't drowned themselves to stay here for yet another day and night."

She followed, latching the door. "I'll go say hello to the cows and will come back to help if Miss Alice starts screaming at all of you for the boys getting dirty."

Jack stopped dead in his tracks. "She screams when she's angry?"

"Not usually." Charlotte gave him a wry smile. "There's always a first time. I'd better go with you to find them. We might have to clean them up without her knowing."

"Thanks for offering, and I hope I don't need your help."

She chuckled. "There's no telling with those two. One minute they're angels. The next, the devil wouldn't take them."

"Let's hurry and see how bad off they are." Jack picked up the pace and peered through the trees, hoping to catch a glimpse of either boy. They reached the water's edge without a single clue about the children's location. "If you were Carter or Conner right now, where would you be?" he asked their sister.

"Next to the stove, desperately trying to get dry before you caught me."

Jack laughed. "I'll bet you're right." He walked with her to the house, steadying her on the slippery parts of the path. "I'll bet you've had a tough time watching over those two."

"Sometimes they get out of hand. The Sisters keep everyone on their best behavior, as does Miss Alice. They don't obey me as much as they do everyone else."

He nodded. Their sister was too young to be an authority to them. He'd been the same to his own brother. "I expect there to be times where I put you in charge. So, they'll have to do what you say when I do."

"If you want them to mind me, they will." She glanced at him with a shy grin. "At least, they'd better."

Jack stepped on the porch and opened the door for her. "Exactly right." He followed her into the house to find the air heavy with tension. The three sat in their usual seats, only Alice eating breakfast. The boys stared at their plates, pushing around the food. Seeing them in his clothes again, he had a good idea of what had happened. Two pairs of pants and socks hung above and to the sides of the stove, water dripping from the hems into buckets.

Alice stood. "Have a seat, and I'll fix your plates." Before Charlotte or Jack could reply, she began dishing out food. The two looked at each other, the silent message being to do as she said, so they eased into their chairs. Neither boy glanced up at them, both still morose.

He broke the uneasy silence first. "All the livestock are fine."

"Good," Alice said. "Boys, eat. Lunch is a long time from now."

They did as requested, taking the smallest bites Jack had ever seen. He raised his eyebrows when Carter looked at him, and the boy grinned until Alice glanced at him. "Breakfast is excellent."

"Of course, it is. You're a terrific cook," she replied.

Jack enjoyed her praise and tried to be modest. "Well, I'm decent."

"Mm-hm. You know you're excellent." Alice returned to the stove with her empty plate. "There's more here, so don't be shy if anyone is still hungry."

Jack hid a smile at how comfortable she seemed in his home. Plus, the positive remark about his cooking didn't hurt. "I might take a little more after you and the kids get your fill."

She turned to him with a smile. "I'm done, but you're right." Alice squeezed more water from the pant legs into the bucket below, saying, "Now's the time for seconds if you all are having any."

Slowly, the three children stood and lined up for more biscuits and gravy with Jack being the tail end. He watched as Alice continued to wring water from the cloth and winked at her when she looked at him. She shook her head, frowning, and went on with her efforts. He couldn't blame her for being frustrated. However, if Alice knew Donovan as well as he did, she'd be calm about the mess, too.

He sat down with his food while she went to the back door with the larger pail in hand. Alice put on her coat, saying, "I'll get some fresh water for washing. Charlotte, begin cleaning up our room in case we can't come back. Boys, I want you to clean up your room as well. Please only pack up what you brought, and that means no toys."

He began to argue, stopping when she shook her head. Jack decided to let the matter rest and nodded when she left the house. Once the door shut, he said, "The toys are only for you three, so they're already yours."

"Can we take them?" Carter asked.

"Let me talk to her first," Jack said. "She's still angry about your clothes."

Charlotte hissed, "What were you two thinking? You knew better, and I told you to be careful."

"We didn't mean to," Carter said.

Conner offered, "He slipped on the bank, and I tried to grab him."

Jack finished the story by saying, "And you both fell in? Then why aren't your shirts wet, too?" Guilt shuttered their faces, and he frowned. "So, you're not being honest?"

"We fell into," Conner said. "Not over into."

"Oh, that's much better," Charlotte quipped. "You two were doing that close to the danger game again, weren't you? One of you stumbles..." She paused when each boy pointed to the other. "It doesn't matter who, and you both end up in trouble." She began clearing the table of the empty dishes. "I hope you both are happy when we're back in the city without a father. Or worse. One's in Chicago, the other in Sacramento, and I'm still in New York. We may never see each other again, thanks to your games."

The boys turned to Jack. Their expressions tugged at his heartstrings. "I'll do what I can to keep that from happening. In the meantime, how about you two do what Miss Alice suggested. You can put everything away later when the adoption goes through, and this is your real home."

They each nodded and went off, the boys into Jack's room and Charlotte into the women's bedroom. He wiped a hand over his face, realizing he hadn't shaved in a day or two. Harry Donovan might be a good friend, but Jack still wanted to look his best when pleading his case as a single parent. He'd also need to file the divorce papers no matter what Alice decided about staying. Ellie was gone, and nothing Jack could do would change her mind. Not after five years of being the best husband he knew how to be. Charlotte's clanking around while packing drowned out any noise the boys made, and he walked into the room to find them seated together on one side of his bed. "You two ready to go?"

"Yes, sir," Conner said in a mumble.

Jack went over and sat next to Carter. "I know you're worried. So am I, but we must have faith things will work out the way we want to. If they don't, then we look for another solution to our problem, all right?"

Carter leaned against Jack, who put his arm around the boy, and then Conner leaned against Carter. The three sat like that for a few seconds until the back door opened. Jack gave the boys a squeeze before removing his arm. "That's our signal to finish up in here and be on our best behavior for Miss Alice. Let's show her how well-mannered you can be as my sons."

His words brought the grins he wanted to see from them, and Jack returned their smiles. "Take your bag out into the main area, and I'll be there in a minute." They did as he asked while he went to his dresser for a razor and the papers. Jack slid the envelopes into his pocket as Alice came into the room. He said, "I'll shave and clean up the kitchen while you pack."

She shrugged. "I never unpacked, so my doing dishes will save us some time."

Her disinterested attitude almost hurt. "So eager to leave, are you?"

Alice followed him out into the living area. "Not as much as wanting to settle things one way or another." She used a dip of her pinky finger to test the large bucket of water heating on the stove before beginning to wash dishes. "I'm anxious to give these three a good home before I leave." She paused in her cleaning. "I'm also ready to deal with any bad news. Get the sadness and hurt over with already and move on."

He looked over at the Hayses. The three were standing at Charlotte's bedroom door, looking much like the sad photograph he had of them from the Home. Alice seemed so calm and matter-of-fact about breaking their hearts; his heart, too. He shoved the folded-up razor into his pocket. "Finish up, get your coat, and meet me in the barn. I need to harness Shep to the wagon and want to talk with you in private before we leave."

Without a backward glance, he grabbed his own coat and left the house. The cold air didn't cool his temper as much as it did his face. His feet crunching on the icy grass drowned out everything but the pounding in his ears. He opened the barn door and went in, pulling the door slightly ajar for Alice.

The hay aroma and soft animal sounds calmed him. He went over to Shep, and the horse came up to him with a nicker. Jack reached out to scratch his forehead. "You're a good one, aren't ya?" A ray of sun showed briefly before Alice closed the door. He didn't look at her. "I'd appreciate it if you didn't continually threaten the children with going back to New York."

"And I would appreciate it if you didn't pretend this adoption was already completed." She walked up to him, her hands in her pockets. "It's not, and there's a good chance it won't be due to Mrs. Dryden's leaving."

His hand fell, and he turned to her. "So, you'll punish all of us for her actions?"

"I'm not." Tears filled her eyes. "I'm just realistic about your chances as a father trying to raise three children on his own."

"Women raise children without a man all the time."

She sniffed. "Do they? Really? No older son who's nearly but not quite eighteen? Or a nearby relative who can check in on them from time to time?" Alice shook her head. "How many women do you know married the closest able-bodied man they could find after the war to keep what little they had?"

He opened his mouth to protest, to say no one married his father after his mother had passed, but Alice was right. His brother had plenty of friends who married a Civil War widow for convenience's sake. Jack hated being wrong, but this time he had to concede. "I see your point." The little hope he'd been trying to hang on to evaporated. "I've been optimistic where you've been realistic, and there's an excellent chance I may never see any of you again." His nose stung as he looked into her eyes. "I don't want to let you go, Alice. Not you or the children." He took her by the shoulders. "I didn't realize how lonely I was, even when not alone, until you all arrived. And now I can't let you go. Not you or any of them."

Tears fell from her eyes as she whispered, "I don't want to leave you, either."

CHAPTER 12

Alice melted into his arms, his comforting hug making the looming verdict far worse for her. "I love you, and I think I have from the first letter you sent us." His hold tightened, and she continued, "I know we've been face to face for mere hours, but I feel as if you've been my friend for years."

His voice low in the dim barn, Jack replied, "I feel the same way. Divorce is supposed to be a shameful thing, and it is to me. But since you've arrived, I consider it a blessing." He leaned back, lifting her chin. "Do you think you'd live closer to Missouri? Closer to here for the children and me?"

She nodded, happiness blooming in her. "I'd love to work out of the St. Louis office, helping orphans from there."

Alice caressed his face, the stubble rough under her fingertips. "They might even expand to Kansas City, and I could be nearby."

Jack scooped her up, twirling her around before kissing her. She clung to him as they gave in to desire until he broke away first. "I need hitch up, or we'll never get to town.

She let go of him, allowing her touch to linger on his arms for a moment. "I suppose the manhunt would start as soon as someone noticed I hadn't returned home."

He laughed while putting the horse's bridle on. "It would, and I'd be hung out to dry." Jack led Shep over to the wagon. "We'll be ready to go in a bit."

"I'll ready the children and grab our bags." Alice paused at the doorway. "If you and Mr. Donovan are truly friends..." She paused when he gave her a stern look. "And I'm sure you are, I'll be the only one not here this evening."

"I didn't know I'd need a plan to keep you with me." He opened the barn door wider. "I'll have plenty to think about while we're riding into town."

"I'll go ready the children." Alice hurried to the house, not surprised to see the trio at the window peering out at her. She couldn't blame them at all for their curiosity. Their fate hung on what adults decided for them.

She stepped inside, asking, "Coats, hats, gloves, and baggage?"

With guilty expressions on all three, they did as ordered, putting on their outerwear. She put on her bonnet and gloves, smiling after finding her bag next to Charlotte's. "Thank you for bringing my things to me."

The girl smiled. "You're welcome. I had to check on the boys and figured it was easier to help you than disturb your talk with Mr. Dryden."

Alice bit her lip at the formality. She couldn't blame her. After this afternoon, they might all be homebound on the next train. She struggled to keep tears from forming in her eyes again. The cook stove held embers, dying ones at that, and she followed the children outside. Jack stood at the wagon's tailgate, helping each child up onto the back. She noticed how he'd piled extra blankets in the wagon bed and smiled at his thoughtfulness.

He turned to her, his eyes bright as he grinned. "There's our fancy Miss McCarthy from town." He reached out to her. "That reminds me. Let me help you up before I go get my hat." Jack went to the side and held out his hand for Alice to take.

She accepted his assistance, settling in on the seat. Alice waited until he came back with his hat on and holding a small bag. She wondered what he'd brought and almost asked until he gave Charlotte the item. The girl grinned at him before glancing at her with a guilty look. Alice added up both guilty looks. "You didn't give them—" she began. "Jack, I specifically told them to leave everything of yours behind."

"Those aren't my toys." He glanced at her and put up his hands, adding, "All right. A few are mine, but I don't know if you've noticed I'm not a boy. Conner and Carter could use the marbles and wooden animals far more than I could."

Alice crossed her arms with a frown at the doll Charlotte held. None of the children looked directly at her, and she knew why. No one wanted to volunteer to behave and leave behind Jack's gifts. She faced forward. If the adoption fell through, they'd either have to discard or bring the gifts to share with all the others. The children knew this, too. "Very well, but no arguing no matter how today turns out for us."

"Yes, ma'am," all three said in unison.

Jack clicked to Shep, and the wagon began moving. They rode down the driveway and down the road a little way. He asked, "How do you get them to behave so well?"

She couldn't help but chuckle at his naivety. Jack would know the answer if he'd had the responsibility of as many children as she had over the past few months. "There are times when they don't. No one can be good every moment."

"True, but then, these three are the best."

She gave him a side glance to see if he were teasing her. His praise of the Hayses was a little too thick to be real. "I don't know if getting soaked in the creek or accepting gifts after being told not to is behaving very well."

He stayed quiet for a few moments. "Very well. Besides those two things, they've been good."

"You're right. They have." She swallowed the lump forming in her throat. "It will be difficult to go home without them." Tears began to form in her eyes, and Alice blinked them back. "But they, you, you'll all be happy, and that's what counts the most."

Jack reached out for her, and she placed her gloved hand in his. The warmth soaked through the layers of leather and thin cotton. The wagon continued and, not trusting her voice, Alice watched as the winter landscape passed by them. The barren trees allowed her to see deep into the woods.

Not even a hint of green announced spring's arrival. She knew her plans for the next five years as recently as three days ago. Alice snuck a peek at Jack. Now? All she wanted to do was make him turn around and take them home.

JACK WATCHED HER FROM THE CORNER OF HIS EYE. SHE fidgeted as restlessly as he felt. One word from her and he'd go back to the farm, drop them off, and drive to town to file anything and everything to keep all four of them with him. Alice might be far too old for him to adopt, but he'd need a governess of some sort, wouldn't he?

He glanced at her again. No, not an employee but a wife. A little chill went through him, unrelated to the arctic air around him. Ellie's leaving should have taught him something about how long forever lasted. Alice sighed, and he couldn't help but smile at the sound. Resisting her would do no good. He'd lost his heart to her already and didn't want it back.

As they rolled closer to Liberty, the cleared land showed more of the established homesteads before the Civil War. He nodded at one of the larger homes and said, "Every time I drive by, that place keeps me going, working harder on my place to make it as grand as theirs." She turned to him with a surprised expression, and he continued, "A foolish dream, I know, but I'd settle for being even half as successful."

"It is inspiring and a beautiful farm." She continued looking at the farm while they drove past. "When did they settle here?"

"A while back. This is the second home. The first was burned down by the Confederates."

"So, they rebuilt," she mused. "Is this home an improvement?"

Jack's automatic answer was "yes" because newer was always better. Still, he sensed her question held a deeper meaning. "Yes. The owners learned from the first and are better builders now." She smiled at him, and he stammered, "Were, I mean since the construction is done and all."

"I see. Do you think they ever miss the old house? Even a little?"

"They might sometimes when remembering the good times they had there."

"That's...understandable." She clasped her hands, staring down at them. "The new building could never truly replace the old in their hearts, I suppose."

He looked behind them to check how preoccupied the children were before taking her hand and giving her a little squeeze before letting go. "I think I'd love the new home so much that I could never give the prior house a second thought."

She blushed, and he had a difficult time resisting the urge to draw her into his arms and kiss her cheeks redder. The traffic picked up, distracting him from embarrassing her with affection. Buggies, wagons, and a stagecoach kept him focused as they neared the town square. The carriages and wagons had increased and, over the noise, Jack asked the children, "See the courthouse? That's where we'll go to finish the adoptions."

The three peered around the adults. Conner tugged on Jack's coat. "Can we go there first and be sure you're our pa?"

Jack looked at Alice, who shook her head, saying, "Sorry, but no. I need to speak to Mr. Donovan about Mr. Dryden's suitability as a parent before anything else." She arched an eyebrow at Jack. "We're going there first."

"Yes, ma'am," he said and tipped his hat. "You're the boss."

"Somehow I doubt that."

He chuckled at her wry expression. Despite the chill, people on their personal missions kept the road crowded. He went straight past the courthouse to his lawyer's office.

With the side road quieter, he said, "Harry is a decent guy, and we've been friends for several years. He helped us—me —file the homesteader's paperwork when we arrived in town."

"Hopefully his decision will be good."

"I'm sure it will be," he responded, leading Shep to the hitching post. Both had been there often enough that the horse remembered what to do. "I'll tie up, and you all can go on in and get warm."

He helped Alice down from the seat. She helped Charlotte, and the four of them went into the office. Jack hurried with securing his animal and the wagon before going inside as well. He walked in just as Donovan came up from the inner office. "Harry. Good to see you."

Donovan gripped his hand in a welcoming handshake. "Jack, you too." He turned to the other four. "I assume these are your children, or soon to be."

"I expect so."

The agent's eyes narrowed, and Alice crossed her arms in response. He took a step forward, saying, "I've met Mrs. Dryden, so you must be Miss McCarthy?"

"Yes, sir, I am. Pleased to meet you."

He frowned and looked from Jack back to Alice. "Do you mind telling me where you've been, young lady?"

CHAPTER 13

ALICE LIFTED HER CHIN. SHE WASN'T GOING TO BE cowed by Mr. Donovan's anger. "I was conducting a suitability visit at the Dryden farm, sir. Mr. Dryden met me at the train station alone, and I thought it best to do an inspection for myself."

"Why, pray tell, would you not take my and several other distinguished citizens' word for Mr. Dryden's reputation?"

"Because circumstances changed..." she started to reply but paused, looking at Jack. Alice didn't want to say the words for him.

He took a step forward. "Because Ellie is gone. She left me before the children could arrive."

"Oh. I see." Still scowling, Donovan went back to his desk chair and sat down. "We're done here, then." He picked up his pen and pulled out a fresh sheet of paper from a drawer. "Nice seeing you, Jack, nice meeting you, miss, and good luck to the children."

A cold wave of horror swept through her. He'd decided their fates in an instant and without concern. She'd go back to New York. The Hayses might be scattered across the United States and territories. Alice didn't know whether to laugh, cry, or rage at the cavalier man's inadvertent cruelty.

"That's all? They can come home with me?" Jack asked.

Donovan barked a laugh. "What? No, of course not." He sat up straighter and resumed his writing. "The four of them are going back home as soon as I can arrange it."

Gasps went out from the children, and she shook her head at them to stay quiet. Charlotte's chin quivered while the boys frowned. Alice couldn't let his decision go without a fight. "Mr. Donovan, are you sure—"

He slid the paper over to Jack as if she hadn't spoken. "This will allow them to stay at the hotel in the event that no train is leaving tonight." He wrote instructions on another note. "And this will guarantee their passage back to the Home."

Alice watched as Jack picked up both papers. She stepped closer to his desk. "Sir, we need to discuss the adoption. The children and I stayed at the Dryden farm for two nights, and I have input on the situation."

He sighed and put his pen down on the blotter. "Tell me, where was Mr. Dryden? In town at the hotel?"

She vowed he wasn't going to shame her. Jack had been a perfect gentleman, and the children had been perfect chaperones. Even if her own behavior was less than stellar. She lifted her chin and said, "Mr. Dryden stayed with us at the farm."

"Do you care about your reputation at all, young lady?" Donovan asked. "Or is staying with a strange man in his home alone something you frequently do?"

"Now look here, Harry." Jack's voice grew louder with each word. "You don't get to talk about Miss McCarthy like that. She's as fine a woman as you'll ever meet." Alice tugged at his shirt, and he glanced back at the children. "She does wonderful work for the orphanage, personally cares for every child, and I can vouch for her sterling reputation."

"I see. How does Ellie feel about her?" He leaned back in his chair with a smirk. "Oh, that's right. She's not here, and you can't adopt as a single parent, now can you?"

She glared at him. It was one thing for this boar of a man to attack her reputation. They'd never met before today. But to besmirch a fine person like Jack, who called this Donovan man a friend? Alice wasn't having it in her presence. "Excuse me, but I beg to differ. You're saying if Mrs. Dryden stayed, you'd let the couple adopt?" Donovan shrugged before nodding, and she didn't let him begin talking. "And if in a year, had Mr. or Mrs. Dryden passed away, you'd then remove the children from their new home despite still having a loving parent?"

"Of course not. By then they'd have settled in and viewed either Dryden as a real caregiver."

Alice narrowed her eyes and leaned in to drive her point home. "And you don't think such a thing could have happened by now? That a person could have passed away before the children arrived?"

"No. Ridiculous." He shuffled papers around as if to appear busy. "I consider only healthy couples, not the sickly ones." Donovan gave Jack a side glance. "Or the ones who continually bicker in my presence, either."

She crossed her arms. Clearly, this man had never lived with anyone else, ever. Even Sister Brigit argued with the bishop sometimes. "Bicker? Really? Are you married?"

"Yes, but what does that have to do with this?"

Ignoring the urge to wipe the smug grin from Donovan's face, she asked, "How long did it take before you knew Mrs. Donovan was your future wife?"

His expression softened at the memory. "From the first moment we met."

She had him trapped, even if he wasn't aware of his position, and asked him, "So, you believe in love at first sight?"

"I do," he began, and his eyes narrowed. "But not in families at first sight."

His argument was weak, and they both knew it. She glanced at Jack while asking, "Excellent term. Why not a family at first sight?" As she said the words his expression relaxed, and his eyes sparkled when she added, "If one can happen, why not the other?"

He stared at the desktop for a couple of seconds. "Dryden, how long have you been divorced?"

"Not long," he began until Donovan glared up at him. "Fine. I have the document in my pocket and will file it as soon as we're done here."

He rubbed his forehead. "You don't make this easy. Miss McCarthy and the children stayed out in the country with you, a single man, and you expect me to believe everything's innocent and proper?"

Jack had been innocent, mostly, and she certainly hadn't been proper at times. Memories of kissing him flooded back and left her cheeks burning. She addressed the Hayses, "Children, please wait outside for a moment; it's important for you to behave." The trio chorused agreement and left the room. Alice turned to Donovan and said, "I do expect you to believe it because it's the truth. Mr. Dryden is an honorable man, and I've represented the Children's Home as well as anyone could."

"So, you relied on the children as chaperones?"

Jack frowned. "We didn't need to rely on anyone. I'm a decent man, and she's a very respectable lady." He leaned forward, putting his hands on his friend's desktop. "Quite frankly, I'm getting real tired of you impugning her reputation."

Donovan stood. "And I'm getting very tired of you both arguing with me. If you think for one second that I'll condone all this, you're both insane." Picking up the second paper, he said, "Take the voucher, go to the hotel, and stay until the next train back." He gave the handwritten sheet to Alice. "This will ensure your trip home." Donovan sat, saying, "Jack, I'm sorry, but we're done here. We're friends, but I also have responsibilities. You'd do the same in my situation."

CHAPTER 14

Jack let Alice leave the room first and followed behind. He could tell the instant the children saw her face. Their expressions changed from hopeful to stricken. His nose stung with the threat of tears over their disappointment and his. He frowned to keep the sadness at bay for their sakes. "Come on now. None of us are giving up. You may be Hayses for now, but that's all." He knelt to the boys' level. "We're going to retreat and regroup. Then, we'll give him no choice but to sign the adoption papers."

"Are you sure?" Charlotte asked before hiccupping a sob. "He didn't like us at all."

As tears began rolling down the girl's face, Alice hugged her. "Now, crying won't solve anything. Mr. Dryden is right. We'll go to the hotel and make up a plan so good no one can refuse us."

He straightened, the boys still clinging to him. "Let's stop by the depot and see when the next train east is. I'm sure they don't run every day."

Alice looked up at him and asked, "Do you think if we had more time to convince him, Donovan would change his mind?"

The hope in her expression tore at his heart. Donovan wasn't a man who waffled on anything. Jack could count on going home alone, again. Still, if he could eke out even one more hour with the children and Alice, he'd do whatever it took. "Trying never hurt anything."

She nodded and let go of Charlotte. "We can visit the train station first." She motioned to the boys. "Come on, pick up your belongings and let's go."

The five of them left the courthouse before Jack remembered the paper burning a hole in his pocket. "Load up, and I'll be back as soon as I can." Before anyone could answer, he turned on his heel and hurried back inside, headed toward the clerk's office.

A young man sat at the desk and looked up when Jack approached. "May I help you?"

He took a deep breath, suddenly nervous. "Yes. I'd like to make my divorce official."

"Divorce?" He stood and reached for the document. "We don't see those every day."

"I'm just lucky, I guess," Jack retorted.

"Hmm." He glanced up from reading. "I know some would agree considering who they're married to." He reached the bottom of the paper and grimaced. "You've signed this already."

"Yes."

He shook his head, still frowning. "You shouldn't have. We'll need witnesses to certify you truly want the action." He began folding up the paper before placing it back in the envelope. "This is unacceptable and will need to be completely redone. A new document with her and her witness's signatures before you can bring it in to us again."

About to point out to the clerk he was wrong, and Ellie hadn't needed witnesses, Jack remembered. Her signature had two smaller names next to hers. She'd done everything correctly, and he'd made a mistake in haste. She would be furious about the extra time and expense. Jack couldn't blame her. He struggled to keep his voice calm. "Very well. I'll see what I can do."

The clerk sat when Jack took the paper back. "I'm sorry, sir. It's the law."

"I understand." He tipped the brim of his hat and said, "Thank you" before turning on his heel and leaving.

While he walked down the hall to where Alice and the children waited for him, his nose stung again. *Damn it all,* he silently cursed. He'd counted on dinner tonight with his new family and planning life around Alice's work and his farm. Jack knew going home alone had always been a possibility. He hadn't expected doing so would be his reality.

He paused in the foyer for a moment, not wanting to go out to them angry. They'd worry, and right now they were all distressed enough without him piling more on them. He stepped aside so another man could leave. Jack watched their faces, hopeful when seeing a male figure at the door, then falling when it wasn't him.

Jack swallowed the lump in his throat. Later tonight, in the hotel parlor after the children were in bed, he and Alice would have to come up with a plan. She was the Home's representative and had to know about some loophole to help him.

He left the building with a smile, grinning bigger when the children looked happy to see him. "Sorry for the delay. Just a little bit of farm business." He climbed up onto his seat, ignoring Alice's searching look at his face. "I hope there's not a train east until next year." He clicked at Shep and snapped the reins. "Who agrees?"

"We do!" the boys shouted and jumped up and down in the wagon bed. "We want to stay forever."

Alice turned and smiled at them, leaning a little against Jack as she said, "No playing while the wagon is moving. Remember?"

"Yes, ma'am." They sat next to Charlotte under the blankets.

Carter hollered, "What's after the train station?"

She turned to talk to them. "The hotel. There might be an eastbound train this evening, so be prepared for disappointment. We might have to go back to New York after all."

The three of them nodded as the wagon creaked to a stop in front of the depot. Jack put a hand on Alice's back. He wanted to pull her into a hug and never let her go. Instead, he said, "Go on inside and get warm while I tie off the horse. If there's a train leaving late tonight, we might be here a while."

She nodded and eased to the ground before helping each child down as well. Jack grinned when noticing how everyone brought his or her bag without needing a reminder. Alice looked up at him and asked, "You'll wait with us?"

Jack didn't understand how Alice could miss his feelings for her. The love he had for her seemed like a part of his soul. "Yes," he said. "I'll stay until you leave."

HIS EXPRESSION APPEARED AS GRIM AS SHE FELT INSIDE. Alice led the children to the depot as the wagon rumbled on to the hitching posts. Their footsteps echoed on the wooden floor. The empty station was a good sign. No bustle meant no train to take them away so soon. Addressing the children, she said, "Have a seat while I check the schedule."

Alice went to the ticket window and examined the chalkboard with train numbers and times scribbled on it. At least three trains were scheduled today. She checked the departure, and her heart sank. One would go west this afternoon, and two left for the east tomorrow morning. Eight in the morning to be exact, and so the five of them had less than twenty-four hours together.

She glanced at the children. All three sat close to each other. Plenty of families between here and New York City would adopt them as a unit. Plus, she'd never been to Oregon and had always wanted to go. Maybe leaving here wouldn't be the worst thing in the world.

The door opened, and she glanced up from the children to the movement. Jack. Her heart did a little flip at the sight of him. Alice gripped her bag tighter. She couldn't buy tickets because getting on the train to leave him was impossible. Oregon had to wait until all of them could travel as a family.

She walked over to Jack before he could reach them. "I want us to speak privately before I settle for going home."

"Of course." He walked past her to the Hayses. "We're going to discuss travel plans and such. Play here if you'd like, but no roughhousing." He looked to Alice for confirmation, and she nodded. Grinning, he added, "No hopping on a boxcar to live like hobos until I get back, all right?"

Charlotte gave him a slight smile while the boys laughed. Alice muttered to him as they walked to the other side of the depot, "You're a terrific father already."

"Thank you," he replied before grabbing her upper arm and pulling her around the corner and up close to him. "You can't leave. They can't leave."

She put a hand on his chest, in part to stop him kissing her and mainly to resist the need to give in to temptation, too. "We may have to go back for a while, Jack. I can't make the rules or break them when things don't go my way."

He scratched under his chin, his movements short and frustrated. "Don't you have the final say-so? Can't you override Donovan's refusal?"

"I can't," she replied before another idea took root in her mind. "But he isn't the only agent we have out here."

"Who else?" He held her by the shoulders. "Why didn't you say so before now?"

"A couple more are in Kansas City proper with several in St. Louis, but I don't know any of them as well as I do Donovan."

Jack muttered a curse, giving her a slightly ornery grin when she gasped. "Sorry. Do I have time to drive down and ask another agent before the next train going east leaves?" He let go of her and walked around the corner to the schedule. "Have you bought the tickets yet?"

She followed, responding, "No, and I need to, but..."

He looked at her and swallowed. "Kansas City's a ways south. Would you be willing to ride to the city with me and ask?"

Alice would do anything for him and the children but hurt them. She had to be honest. "Yes, but Jack, there's a strong chance he'll have the same opinion as your friend and refuse the request."

His eyebrows met in the middle of his forehead, and he pinched the bridge of his nose. "Are you saying you don't want me to try? I won't drive down there if you don't want to stay. You all can go home, and I'll keep trying to adopt Charlotte and the boys until I can't anymore."

Tears filled her eyes. "I'm sorry. I'm being a coward, afraid of hearing him refuse you, too. I don't want to hear anyone else tell you we can't be a family." She looked from him to the children. The trio sat silent, listening. Alice reached for a handkerchief from her bag but ended up wiping her eyes with her sleeve. "Fine. We have to present your case before tomorrow morning's deadline, so let's get started."

He picked her up in a hug and swung her around with a whoop. "You sure do know how to make a bad day better, little lady." Jack went to the children. "You heard her. We're going to Kansas City. Think you can find Shep for me?"

Conner hollered, "Watch us, Pa! We'll bring him up for you."

Both boys ran out of the depot and Charlotte grabbed their carpetbags with hers. She walked up to the couple. "Now that they're gone, you can tell me the truth, and I won't cry or tell the boys. Are we going to Kansas City to take the next train east because tomorrow morning isn't soon enough?"

Jack took the bags from her. "Let me get those, and no. We're truly going there to talk to another agent. I'm not giving up on you three. Not until I'm forced to do so."

Charlotte tilted her head, as if not quite believing him. "What about Miss McCarthy? Will you let her leave us, too?"

"I can't speak for her." He looked over at Alice. "She's her own woman and all I can do is hope she moves to one of the Missouri orphanages to continue her work."

Charlotte gave him a sly grin, and Alice braced herself. That expression always landed the girl in trouble. Wanting to head off any faux pas at the pass, she spoke up first. "There they are, in the wagon already." She turned to the younger girl. "You first and I'll follow."

She did as instructed, climbing up and over to where her brothers were. Jack handed them their bags, and they rushed to grab their toy animals. Carter said, "We can make bigger fields and have races on the way there."

"Yeah!" Conner responded, and both shuffled around in the back, wobbling the wagon as Alice settled in on the wooden seat. Jack followed and clicked at Shep.

Charlotte knelt, moving to squeeze in between the two adults. "You know, if you and Miss McCarthy were married today, all our problems would be solved."

CHAPTER 15

"Charlotte Simpson Hays! Whatever possessed you to say such a thing?"

Jack laughed at the young girl's cheeky grin and winked at her. "It's a fair statement. We're both good-looking and have our health."

Alice frowned at him. His making light of such impertinence only encouraged their unruliness. She needed to get all four of them under control. "You're not helping, Mr. Dryden. Not at all."

By now, the boys had discarded their toys and flanked their sister. Conner said, "Char is right. You two should get married so we can be adopted."

Conner nodded. "Then, you'd already have all the children you'd need."

"No babies necessary," his brother added.

Jack glanced at Alice with a grin before staring straight ahead. "Now, no more of this. It takes time for a couple to meet, court, and decide to marry. Even if we were meant to be together, two or three days isn't long enough for such a decision."

"He's right." She faced the front as well. The three of them might as well know all the facts so they didn't spend the hours to Kansas City pestering them. "Besides, he's still married; a remarriage isn't possible at the moment."

The children sat back on their heels, each giving a disgusted groan. Alice tried to hide her smile over their reaction. Jack leaned over, touching her shoulder with his and whispered, "I signed the paper and tried to file it at the courthouse."

"Just now?" she whispered back. Jack had wanted to be single so soon? Alice had to learn more and asked, "What happened?"

He shrugged. "The clerk needed witnesses. Since I'd already written my name, he wouldn't take the signature as mine."

Alice frowned. She'd witnessed several adoption signings and knew most of the tricks needed for remote farm families. "You didn't sign your name again on a blank piece of paper with witnesses for them to compare the two?"

Jack looked over at her in amazement. "No, and I didn't think to ask. The clerk didn't offer."

"Hmm, he must be new or inept." Alice sat up a little straighter, determined to give the official a piece of her mind when they returned to Liberty. "Either way, I've had to compare signatures several times. People get anxious, not willing to wait, and sign before anyone thinks to call in the witnesses to verify."

He glanced back at the children for a few moments. Staring at her, he said, "Alice, if I turn around, get the witnesses, and file the divorce, will you marry me? Today?"

She looked into his eyes for a few seconds, stunned. Marriage? "Today?" she squeaked before clearing her throat. "I mean, we can't possibly be married today." The hopeful expression faded from his face, and she hastened to add, "Later, maybe, when I have my employment moved to Missouri or even stopped altogether. I do hate to give up my good works."

Alice glanced back at the children who all sat still and silent, waiting for her final answer. Each child wanted her to marry Jack. Goodness knows, she did, too. Except, she didn't want to refuse Jack outright before asking for more time for a real courtship and cause them to lose their chance at a forever home. She looked back at his handsome profile. He'd been so very kind to the youngsters, wanting to give them a good home. His eyes sparkled whenever he looked at them or her, and the kiss they'd shared? Pure heaven.

Jack smiled. "I'd like for us to help with whatever you need to continue with your work. As long as you're with us, that's really all we ask."

She loved this man, the children he wanted to adopt, and might as well admit the truth to everyone here. Unable to stop them, her feelings tumbled out of her as she put a hand on Jack's arm. "Yes. If you love me, I'll marry you."

The war whoops from the others startled Shep and Alice alike. Jack pulled the horse to a halt and hugged her with the children following his example. He said, "Crazy woman. Of course, I love you. Just promise me you'll work through any problem we have before planning to leave me. That's all I ask."

She leaned back to look at him, giving a reassuring smile to his worried face. Caressing his cheek, Alice responded, "I promise." She put a finger over his lips to keep him from answering too quickly. "You won't mind if I have to go back east a time or two to help others whenever I can?"

He kissed her fingertips, and she chuckled at the tickle when he said, "You can travel the world as long as you always come home to me."

"Us," Charlotte added. "Come home to all of us."

Alice looked down at her and caught the boys nodding in agreement. She laughed and said, "Then maybe we should turn around and catch up on some paperwork to make us a family."

"You heard the lady, Shep." Jack tugged on one of the reins. "Time to go home." He took one of her hands in his. "Our home."

THANK YOU FOR READING JACK AND ALICE'S LOVE story! If you enjoyed this book, please consider sharing the love and leave a review. Check out the About the Author section for more information on keeping in the loop on new books for you.

Continue reading for an excerpt from Lost Orphans, the next book in the American West-Orphan Train series.

Harry Donovan locked up his law practice. Closing earlier than usual, he wanted to enjoy the beautiful spring day. His late wife, Polly, would have loved the fresh rain smell lingering in the air. She'd have sat at her desk in his law office, staring out at the extra bustle of farmers in town buying seeds. The keys jingled on their way to the bottom of his pocket. Her death still ached in his heart. His hand hesitated over the doorknob. He weighed what he *should* be doing with a free afternoon versus what he *wanted* to do.

Fishing it is, he decided, before heading toward the general store. Even though he kept a fishing pole at home, Polly would never let him bring worms into the house. He strolled down the boardwalk. Various people either greeted him warmly or gave him the cut. He returned the kind words and laughed off the others. Being considered a good guy or bad guy never bothered him as long as justice was served. Fairness sometimes cost him but was worth it in his mind.

He pushed open the general store door. Entering the building, he blinked a few times, unaccustomed to the darker interior. The new shopkeeper kept busy, helping another customer. Harry walked over to the few books on a shelf. A couple of children, a young boy and a younger girl, passed slim books back and forth between them. The two seemed familiar, but he'd placed so many orphans from the trains that he couldn't remember for sure who they were.

"We did read this one, remember? At the other place," the girl argued.

"No, Mama Yvette read it to us." The young boy held up a slim volume to her. "This is from that home."

The girl pushed the book back to him. "I don't want to read it."

"Me neither." The boy tossed it back on the shelf. "Not unless Mama Mellie reads the story to us."

Mama Yvette? The uncommon name must mean Yvette Robinson. Of course, now he could place the children. They'd been sent back by one couple for not being hard workers, and he'd found them a new home. The Robinsons took them in last year, nearly a couple of months before Polly passed away. He looked from them to the only other adult customer in the store to see if either parent was here. "Hello, Liam and Gracie, is it?"

The children stopped poring over the books and stared at him. The boy stepped in front of his sister. "It is. Have we met?"

"You don't remember?" Harry asked, feeling a bit guilty for asking because recognizing them had taken him a moment, too. He offered, "I helped your parents adopt you last year."

The two glanced at each other before looking at the approaching woman. "Sorry, mister, but it's been a while. We've been busy with school, church, and the farm."

After the woman came up to the three of them, she looked from Harry to Liam. "I hope they weren't bothering you, sir." The girl hid behind the woman, pulling the skirt around her like a cloak.

"Not at all." He tried to do anything but stare at the red-haired beauty in front of him. She stood a little shorter than he did, with a lovely figure despite the loose brown dress. Her eyes were darker than he'd expected a woman with her coloring to be. Most women with vibrant hair wore sunbonnets to protect their very fair skin, too. He wanted to reach out and let a stray curl of hers wind around his fingers, to see if the copper shimmered in the light. One of her eyebrows rose. He stopped staring and cleared his throat. "I handled their adoption for the Robinsons." The flash of fear in her expression puzzled him. Her nervous mannerisms stirred his suspicions. True, he hadn't been to visit in a while, but surely someone would have notified him of any changes. "Is everything all right?"

She laughed and gave a little wave as if shooing a fly. "Yes, yes, of course. I didn't realize how important of a role you played in Liam and Gracie's lives. Thank you for finding them a home here in Missouri."

Harry didn't want to believe a woman with such a kind face could lie, but he'd seen it happen time and again. Her answers appeased his concerns, but not much. Prodding her for more information in case he needed to act as an official adoption agency representative, he asked, "What about the Robinsons? Are they nearby?"

She and the children exchanged a glance before she reassured him. "Oh, no, they're out of town for an extended stay. Yvette's mother became ill, and Matthew didn't want to leave her alone or take the kids in case of infection."

"Ah, very well." Her answer reassured him far more than her body language did. Using the couple's given names implied a friendship, certainly. Still, he didn't have a thriving law practice by relying on assumptions. "How do you know the Robinsons, again?"

"We're neighbors. My husband and I," Her slight smile faded. "I mean, *I* have a farm adjacent to theirs."

Her answer surprised him, so he blurted out, "Just you?"

The woman twisted her shopping bag handles. "Yes. Sadly, my husband passed away in the last sickness."

No wonder she was nervous. A single woman taking care of two children and a farm? There was a reason he never placed orphans with either a man or woman on their own. He firmly believed children needed two parents at home. "I'm sorry for your loss."

"Thank you." She stared down at her shopping bag. "He was good with farming and such. His prior work is helping me to succeed now."

"Good. I'm glad you're able to continue on." His reply sounded stilted even as he said the words. She nodded and he almost offered help, to be a good person, of course. But his farming days belonged to his childhood. Besides, the children's care and happiness should be his primary focus, not their lovely neighbor. He smiled at the two youngsters. They'd been watching the conversation as if the adults had been passing a ball back and forth. "So, Liam, Gracie, are you behaving well for Mrs..."

"Nelson."

He waited for her to permit him to use her first name, but when she didn't, he squatted to the girl's eye level. "Mrs. Nelson, then. Not giving her any trouble, I expect?"

"No, sir," the boy replied. "We like living with her. She takes care of us real good and doesn't make us cry. Right, Gracie?"

The little girl peeked out from behind Mrs. Nelson's skirt and nodded. Harry straightened into standing again. He couldn't help but grin at her adorable and small face. "Very good. You both look well, which is a testament to your parents and Mrs. Nelson's care."

Mrs. Nelson smiled at him, genuinely. "Thank you, Mr..."

"Donovan," he supplied.

"I appreciate your approval, sincerely. We do need to start for home." She gave him a small nod. "Farm chores don't reward those who linger in town, no matter whose company a person is enjoying."

"I'll be by your or the Robinsons' farm later on in the week," Harry offered. "There are a few court appearances I need to make, but once they're done, I'll be free to do a health and welfare check on the children."

She put a hand on Liam's shoulder. "I see. We'll be ready then. Have a good day, sir. Children?"

Gracie held onto Mrs. Nelson's skirt as they left the store. Harry watched as the three of them passed by the front windows and disappeared from sight. Others walked in, the doorbell ringing with each entry. He moseyed over to the wooden tub full of dirt and fishing worms. Most people dug their own bait. Living in Liberty, Missouri, meant he didn't have the time or space to find worms. He dug around for the best nightcrawlers, mulling over how well the children seemed. Life with the Robinsons agreed with them. They had a little bit of color from playing in the sun. Their clothes were clean and pressed. Liam's face, as well as what he saw of Gracie's, had filled out with regular meals.

Harry picked out the worms most likely to catch fish, setting them aside. When he rode out to evaluate the two children's home again, he'd need to ask when the couple left. Mrs. Nelson clearly deserved some of the credit for the children's thriving. She'd been a widow as long as he'd been a widower. He ran his fingers through the pan of soil. Sometime, he'd need to talk with her, ask how she dealt with the long lonely days.

He stopped cold. Was he lonely? Yes, of course. Without Polly, everything rang with an emptiness. Yet, he'd expected the sadness from losing her. He took a rag from a nearby stack and placed his choice worms on the fabric. Meeting a pretty woman didn't mean he was lonely. All he wanted was a visit with her, nothing special. The children needed a health and welfare check, too, an excellent reason to see her home. They'd talk about how she coped on a farm without farmhands, assuming she hadn't hired any. Asking about others in her employ or courting her would be a substantial question to ask. For the children's sake, of course.

Continue reading Lost Orphans on Amazon

ABOUT THE AUTHOR

With an overactive imagination and a love for writing, I decided to type out my daydreams and what if's. I currently live in Kansas City with my husband and a few cats. When not at the computer, I'm supposed to be in the park for a jog and not buying everything in the yarn store's clearance section.

Find me online at:

https://twitter.com/LauraLStapleton

https://www.facebook.com/LLStapleton

and at http://lauralstapleton.com.

Subscribe to my newsletter to keep up on the latest and join my Facebook group at Laura's Favorite Readers.

Made in United States
North Haven, CT
16 May 2022

19217306R00114